PEOPLE WITH A DIFFERENCE

107 anecdotal stories to tickle your mood

notionpress.com

PEOPLE WITH A DIFFERENCE

107 anecdotal stories to tickle your mood

Shamsher Kendal

notionpress.com

Notion Press

Old No. 38, New No. 6

McNichols Road, Chetpet

Chennai - 600 031

First Published by Notion Press 2016

ISBN 978-93-5206-716-9

Contents

Foreword

By Prof. Amrit Lal Madan

(A Prolific writer who has written nearly fifty books of poetry, drama and novel.)

Very few writers in Haryana have really endeavored to write anecdotes or mini stories in English. The reasons are obvious, one of which is the difficulty of portraying true colours of Haryanvi milieu including her typical characters and witty dialogues. In this regard I can remember only two names, one is that of Mr. Rajbir Deswal who has for long dominated the scene in The Tribune, and the other is Mr. Madhukant of Rohtak who has brought out an anthology of his mini stories titled 'The Empty Frame'.

Now I have this anthology of anecdotal stories penned by Mr. Shamsher Kendal who belongs to my own area of Kaithal Haryana and is like Mr. Deswal an ex-student of R. K. S. D. College. The anecdotes are almost true, tinged with the imagination of a narrator who has given them artistic treatment, bringing out the elements of humour, irony and hilarity, as of innocence.

These anecdotes are sure to provide the readers glimpses of Haryanvi countryside and a peep into the hearts and minds of its people. They will be both amused and thrilled at the common village scenes and the robust rustic activities like village urchins holding tough group competitions and a sobbing bride being given a hearty send off by singing women, while an ogler stood watching in a corner as in 'A Departing Girl'.

In Villages a car howsoever old, is still a show piece of immense prestige and pride. What if it is started like a tractor emitting a lot of smoke and noise while children stand watching and clapping as in 'A Used Car'.

The influential villagers, conscious of their political position; particularly the Panchayat Pradhans who are accompanied by their stooges wherever they go. But when they are caught drinking at a wayside dhaba by a police raiding party, they flee the scene as is depicted in 'Political Boasting'.

The villagers in Haryana often indulge in litigations over small matters. But soon they get tired of going to court for hearings. They may even share the same bicycle while doing so or even prefer imprisonment to long distance walks, as in 'Travesty of Justice'.

In another anecdote depicting a common village scenario we find cleaning up of a choked channel through voluntary service rendered by groups of villagers. But if a villager who remained absent from service is awarded with sweets instead, how he reacts is quite funny as in 'Desilting the Watercourse'.

Sometimes a breach of a set daily routine results in some unexpected awards. One such incident sends its readers into peals of laughter in 'It Was Porridge'.

We can also find school going kids being settled in a pedal cart like the green grocery and being showered with parting kisses by their doting young mothers even if they are yelling as in 'The Lovely Kids'.

These are some of the anecdotal examples chosen at random wherein the observant narrator is adding his own pithy and witty comments to make the reading more enjoyable. I hope the readers will not only enjoy reading these true stories but also develop insights into the working of hearts and minds of these innocent people.

Prof. Amrit Lal Madan

PREFACE

When a famous person says something very commonplace thing, it becomes special but when a peculiar thing is done by a common man it either goes unheard or taken without warmth. Despite the peculiarities people attach significance to greatness of a person. The book 'People with a Difference' is unique in itself because we talk about more about such persons in our conversations, who live or lived around us and did something in an uncommon way and sometimes incongruities come to the fore and these things become worth talking. Such people carry much substance in a particular region because to be an issue of gossiping is far better than living a life of non-entity. People of such genre attract immediate attention locally, in comparison to the widely known personages.

I am highly grateful to Mr. Rajbir Deswal a celebrated author and illustrious columnist who gave me a substantial push by jotting down a valuable comment on my crude story 'The Tufty Boy' and some other anecdotes. I sincerely behold my parents who bestowed me a life of sovereign flights. I am indebted to my English teachers Mr. Ramnnath and Prof. S. K. Garg who strengthened me at the foundation level. Prof. Amrit Lal Madan, my esteemed teacher and a widely known figure in literature, condescended to write the foreword of this book, his esteemed contribution is unforgettable.

My thanks also go to Mr. Jagbir Nandal, Mr. Rajpal Punia, Prof. Sucha Singh Sandhu, Prof. Jaspal Malik, Principal Bhupinder, Principal Harbansh, Mr. Suresh Yadav and a lot more who appreciated continually my writings even at fledgling level.

On the whole I haven't mentioned any name in my short stories but there are a few characters which were necessary to be titled. Such names are general names and do not indicate to any particular person. Reading George Orwell extensively and intensively helped me a lot to step forward towards writing. I think he introduced openness and liberty in selecting a topic and genre of one's choice in prose writing.

Shamsher Kendal

CHAPTER 1

1. THE LOVELY KIDS

The beauty of the morning is credited with so many factors like the pleasing atmosphere, lesser din, clean and fresh mind and lively feelings. Beautified and embroidered children waiting for the school bus on the city roads also enhance the idyllic milieu. There evolve a pattern of colourful dresses. Many of such children make use of this period in some sort of sports, without worrying about the laboriously prepared uniforms and others in prankster activities. But the most charming scenes are there where nursery kids are bidden farewell by the young mothers, parting with their innocents, invoking delightful emotions on their faces. While returning from the green belt, these packs of scholars standing at every stoppage waiting for the vehicles attract me; the tincture of the uniforms also changes, due to numerous educational institutions.

I occasionally come across a pedaling cart, beautifully furnished and decorated for the younger ones. Slenderized benches are arranged parallel, kids are sitting facing each other, and due to their tiny sizes they cuddle in dozen. They make an attractive pattern like in the green grocery shop, washed vegetables placed in rows. Some of them seem sullen and heavy hearted because of the sudden alterations in their daily itinerary, a few are distinguishable enough shining in upbeat mood and hardly affected by the positioning. I strode myself to keep a pace with their pedaling cart feigning ignorance of them and tried to get their lovely innocent conversations. One was trying to convince a yelling kid, "Now, we have to go daily, and not to come in mid time and also not to weep." (ab har roj Jana hai, bich mein nahin aana, aur rona bhi nahin hai).

2. Fruit Temptations

I procrastinated my first visit to Pinjore Garden many times thinking it as a mere park and to go specially to see a parkland is meaningless. But lately while coming from Shimla we stopped at Pinjore to have a look at the Pinjore Garden. It is simply gorgeous, fabulous and unique. Beautiful fruit trees are planted in attractive straight lines. Several types of fruit trees are grown in different segments. Stylish fountains and colourful lights are enhancing its pleasing charms. Same sort of plantation is at Kurukshetra Horticulture Garden in a HUDA sector, particularly chikoo trees in seven acres area out of nearly twenty acres where several types of fruit trees are flourishing. These are catering to the nutritional needs of the city and adjoining region. But it is not developed for commercial and tourism purpose, though thousands of people visit Kurukshetra annually as tourists.

Likewise there are around two hundred jamun trees in green belt park of HUDA Kaithal. In the month of July these trees are full of savoury fruits and catch your attention when you stroll through it. Last Sunday I rose leisurely and still thought to saunter in the park for a short period. l was traversing the serpentine pathway covered by the jamun arbors. Appealing bunches of fruits were just luring me. I saw back and forth to see if anybody wasn't watching me and hurled a slipper towards the cluster of fruits. My slipper entangled between the branches and the foliage. My priority shifted to get free my slipper leaving my desire of shaking off some Jamuns. I hurled my second slipper to free the first one. To my dismay it also got caught by the dense tree. It doubled my predicament and felt perturbed. Then the watchman, a Nepali came for my help saying, "kya jarurat thi babuji (was it needed)." Otherwise I had to go home barefooted.

3. Stray Dogs

The pattern of things even of the fauna alters when you move from the village to a town. Even the street dogs are discernible and recognized by the village folks; vice versa these docile creatures also demonstrate their affection towards the human beings by swaying and sometimes sticking their curved tails between the hind legs. They have given them special funny names on the basis of their hues and complexions, like blacky, chalky, browny, husky, dusky, hazel etc. Some are named on their characteristics and behavior. These dogs often respond on the pleasing sounds mouthed by a person. Of course they are not tamed but can be categorized as partially tamed. Coexistence and mutual understanding is watchable in a pastoral environment. Even the expectant mother bitches and lactating mother bitches are taken care of; people provide them the requisite provisions and nutrition.

In routine the stray dogs are also attached to different households and reach there at the meal hours, and people cater them their share of food. They might be seen in the foyer crouching and lolling their tongues while you dine. In towns and cities the scenario is different, there exist mutual indifference and distrust between the humans and the canines. On my walkway in the morning two groups of dogs stretch themselves. The first one seems more attentive and seen growling with minority members. The second party strikes after walking one and half kilometers on the wider road and their demeanor is what the flying squad generally writes in the visitors book, of course peaceful. The sensual factor might be prevailing.

4. A Smart Hawker

In the morning there is a special spectacle of the vegetable vendors. Different types of conveyances are engaged in this activity. I see first a tractor trolley which is like a locomotive shop, the trolley covered by a tarpaulin, one person sitting at the rear end to weigh off the veggies like bitter gourd, bottle gourd, apple gourd, garlic, ginger, peas, onion etc. the other drives it at different places, simultaneously helping the weighing person by passing on different items and he also announces their arrival in the street. Though they use a loud speaker for announcing their arrival in the avenue but people are accustomed to the sound of the raised silencer. Then there comes a three wheeler with a ruffling sound of its engine and body. After some time there arrives a mule cart with tapping, the seller standing straight on it, handling the leash. He is a solo player, shouts loudly to announce his appearance in a habitation, enumerates names of vegetables in a rhythmic way which he is carrying and instantly turns to his weighing balance on seeing a purchaser. He also mouths special voices to move and halt his mule.

Pedaling carts and also pushing carts are also hauled strenuously. They demonstrate their presence by striking a metal with handlebars, by resounding a bell or mostly by yelling in a specific manner. One day I heard two voices of the vegetable sellers, one loud enough and the other some squeezed out. I came out of the house to buy some green foodstuffs. There was a single vendor with his pushcart. I searched the other but nobody was in sight. Anyhow I completed my purchases. Later in another street I noticed the same veggie vendor named Ruldu whom I recognized, shouting twice in different voices. I asked him why he was dramatizing all these things and he confided me that he was doing so in order to exhibit a feign competition to draw the people out of their houses. Isn't Ruldu a smart guy?

5. Menace of Stray Cattle

Stray cattle on the busy roads have become a menace. The stranded cows may be seen straggled in midst of the road, chewing the cud, unconscious about the city's whirligigs and zigzags, impeding the speedy vehicles. Often carefree bike riders got struck, getting injuries and even jeopardizing life in some instances. Even sincerely driving people meet accidents by such vagabond zebus. Calves suddenly may leap upon you from the road dividing hedges. Not only the sitting cows but fighting bulls, growling dogs, gibbering and screeching monkeys all are contributing in the driving perils. Nobody is safe when one is out on the road, be they the children, the youths or the elderly people. Easy preys are the weakest, generally we hear the cases of bitings by the warm blooded animals like dogs and monkeys and then ensues the rabies treatment, regular injections that costs hefty expenses.

In the morning today such situation arose, but harm was aborted. In the green belt I was walking on the serpentine strip with a brisk pace. An air force retiree joined me; I slowed down my pace to keep in tandem with the jovial respected gentleman. Then we halted on the sudden deflection to see a monkey who was screeching, surrounding and threatening the beleaguered dog, who was sticking his tail between the hind legs. More walkers stopped to see, most of them wanted to save themselves from the onslaughts of the beasts. Soon they were shoved away by the persistent pelting and debate began about the strayed cattle problem. Everyone was holding the villagers responsible. Due to overuse of machinery in agriculture the bullocks have turned redundant and unaffordable. People gather them in large numbers and march towards the towns to leave them there. An octogenarian in peculiar attire of a rural folk responded, "You, in majority left the villages without bringing with you your share of fauna, they will surely pursue you."

CHAPTER 2

6. It was Porridge

Man's life can be equated with a train which runs on a fixed track and at fixed time, and it is not uncomplicated to bust the routines and subroutines. The life path is so much orbicular that any attempt to infract it, seems unsafe, hazardous and perilous. We may find ourselves entwined to roundish routines and habits. If you are a frequent train passenger, you see at a crossing people halted, eagerly waiting the passing of the train, you can recognize the faces that approach there daily at fallen bars. On your music system you have a good collection of songs of every hue, and numerous but as the first number completes, your mind activates to tell the ensuing song even before hearing the next tune, everything seems to be mechanical, happening consciously or unconsciously. Your round the clock itinerary is orderly placed, even of the morning chores, your bitten path, your stroll friends, your rest benches, your wardrobe even your swaying the shaving brush on the chin to form soapsuds. Timing for the breakfast and later meals, the ingredients are customized and procedural.

Some of the cycles are natural but some are espoused. Probability of breach of routine arose when I was alone at home nearly for a week, I took liberty from the routine pace and pattern, drifted from the early rising, stayed away from the customized apparels and even skipped the three times meal and prescribed items. Autonomy again jerked when an acquaintance began rendering the meal box three times in spite of my consistent refusing. One evening when I was leaving for a walk, the uncle appeared with tiffin and he also informed me that it was a plain meal that day. I thanked him and said that I preferred simple and plain repast. He again insisted on its plainness once more. On return I also planned to deviate from trampled aisle and bought brewski, savoured the liquid till late. For supper, I uncorked the meal box, was astounded to see the meal which was repeatedly being claimed simple, was more than plain, it was porridge.

7. The Dipsos

On the whole I don't drink but I don't hate drinkers even revelers and boozers. I myself don't miss the opportunity if circumstances are so conducive and favourable. Many a time I pass my evenings among the dipsos. They make the arrangements meticulously, within time their table is well stocked with washed glasses, seltzer, mineral water, eatables and well packed whiskey bottle that comes last. They open it in a stylish manner with a feeling of pleasure on their faces. They make the first peg fast. l often relish the eatables they offer, particularly salad and fruits. I bask their conversations, they're rarely critical of anybody. Their respect, their courtesies are unmatched and unparalleled. Nobody is as social as a reveler. But they are always afraid of the altercations with their spouses. Fear always prevail among them of the affray at home as everybody have, including the teetotaler. Often their talks are elevated enough, they even plan to coup a democratically elected government but when time comes to go home, their fervency comes down. Broadly they are in favour of fraternity and tranquility in society.

I observe, different drinkers behave differently after engulfing a peg. One proceeds on morality and humanity talks, second ventures on famous sports personality of a particular region, third tries to divert all towards humour and hilarious things, but most popular issue always remains politics, they seldom take anything profoundly. One of them, who seems confused to listen multiple issues simultaneously, considers them prattlers. He habitually articulates the line, 'Oh God, have mercy on this world', after each peg. I noticed him saying the particular line three or four times. Then I requested him, "Sir, winter has come, your line should be altered to, 'Oh God have jersey on this world', if you please."

8. Doctor Sahab

Teachers are taken as role models; students are highly impressed by their worthiness, their knowledge and their sublime approach. The seniors are also not taken less; they are also esteemed by the juniors particularly at higher level. They are called doctor shahabs and some are quite discernible for their ability and accomplishments and leave imprints on your mind. Another thing is that they are at hand and their advice and guidance is advantageous and treasured. I recollect a guy who was a senior but not from my faculty. He was doing doctorate in Economics. On casual assemblages like at canteen or in retiring room his points and facts were impressive enough on any issue, be it social, political or on economy. He had a great grasping on politics and political people. He challenged everything by quoting someone. My relationship with him developed into cordiality. Sahab was dropped after some time and I called him doctor only.

At one of debates we were also invited by him and the topic was about the role of rural banks and their impact on farming community. In spite of micro financing, why the farmers are in miserable conditions? Different speakers put their points like the corruption at public sector, less awareness in farmers about the government schemes, improper use of advances by the rural folks. But doctor's concepts were special on this issue. He illustrated it with best example. He said that a person had a tooth ache, people suggested him many remedies, one of the remedies was applied accordingly, and lumps of pudding (halwa) were placed on the aching tooth to relieve the pain as was suggested. But as soon as a lump was placed he gulped it, then another was tried, it also went down in the same way. He continued gulping the lumps and the remedy became meaningless. Then someone suggested that the guy should eat pudding freely and satisfactorily, and then the lumps could be sustained on the aching tooth. He said it was clear that the farmers consumed the loan amount on other things like constructing the house, on marriages etc. but these are needed. Such loans should also be given to achieve the requisite goals. The doctor's facts were illustrious and also practicable.

9. Supremacy of Wives

Once my friend whose relative was a district head of police told me a curious thing and that defies the general adage 'you are an officer only for your family members'. The police officer was my friend's brother in law, his sister's husband. The district head manages, handles and controls all law and order situation of a region. He is powerful enough and a man of authority, everyone considers so but at home he is as layman and hapless as other common people of the society. My friend told that one night his brother in law came home, the official residence, late at night after drinking too much. The pilot security departed after leaving the officer at the main entrance of the residence and there were other policemen for the night duty. He told further that when the officer knocked inner gate of the house, his sister refused to open the door for her drunkard husband. He looked around vexedly, and found himself in a predicament. If he went out, the guards at the gate would come to know the truth, the restrictions by the wife, and she was in no mood to open the door, he passed the night in the veranda on a wooden cot 'takhhat'. Crux is that the wives hold the ultimate authority.

One day I was attending a revelers company, their debate, and their talkfest is interesting enough, they start from the municipality level, then state politics, the national scenario, the hike in dollar price and role of America in Gulf countries' violence. I think they should certainly be included in policy making at some level. At every issue their assertion is watchable, but as the time passes, night advances, get late to reach at home, their fervour begins coming down. That night I went with one of them, the host, to leave him to his house on my bike. It was late night; the guy requested me to halt fifty metres from his house and also told me to wait for some time. I saw him walking to the door of his house, and knocking. I listened dimly; his wife was shouting at him incessantly and was not interested in opening the door. He returned back and got promise from me, the matter not to be disclosed to anybody, whispered, "Would you provide me a cot." (manjha mil jega).

10. Man of Clear Concepts

Whenever I see him after two or three days, someone new is accompanying him, somebody strange to me, walking with him. People finds his company cordial as well as refreshing, even a few moments passed with him would prove instrumental in enhancing one's intelligence. Yes, he is a learned magnetic personality, a man of cognition. He touches a wide range of issues with intensive and extensive details. If he speaks on sports, would enlist the famous sportspersons of a particular game and who have touched the height, If he dwells upon the issue of farming, his facts are unmatched and unparalleled, tells even about the entomology and test weight of a cereal, the suitable climate, deciduous and non-deciduous plants. If economy is discussed, he will start from the cottage and small scale industries, their significance, the employment prospective and their technology.

But more people are interested to listen to him on politics; he has an exceptional grasp on this subject, elaborates the history of frontrunners, the trailers but never comes on vilification or vituperation. He no longer talks about communism but still has a soft corner for the people of such thinking. He is a good psephologist, during elections he is most sought after guy, the wagerers are seen contacting him and seeking his advice about the winnability. His style of narration, his enunciation is marvelous, people are simply attracted to listen to him and above all he is a highly social fellow. I always try to extract something interesting and newfound out of him and relish his fellowship. Occasionally he tends to be imbiber and sometimes even before the fall of night. One day I advocated and pleaded him that it was not fair to take the booze before dusk. But his repartee was also amusing. He said, "Mr. There is no night for four months in Norway, how long they would wait to fuddle."

CHAPTER 3

11. Desilting the Watercourse

To work collectively had its own pleasure. It was time when there was not sufficient agricultural machinery and people accomplished any work with mutual cooperation. Just before the rainy season we had to desilt the watercourse, for it became choked with earthy matter, sand and muck due to flow of water most of the time. Weeds also overgrew in thickets along the banks of the channel. It was virtually the preparation for plantation of paddy crop. The silted up watercourse was to be cleared enough to make it streaming unhindered, to have sufficient supply for the water hungry paddy plants. It was a common cause and everyone whose farm got supply from the stream had a duty to desilt the watercourse once a year, thus it was a cumulative project. At least one person had to work from each farm for one day to remove silty materials. If someone doesn't turn up from a family he had to provide a few rupees as amercement. That day I was a part of the watercourse digging team.

There were more than thirty persons carrying spades including me and everyone was assigned a stretch of nearly ten feet to clear up the channel. I saw everyone doing the job with full jocularity, digging and throwing the spadesful muck outside in the fields. After finishing the ten feet patch, one had to move to another length to clean up. The whole watercourse was desilted before noon. Then all sat together to have a feast of sweets which was purchased out of amercement money, collected from the absentee farmers. After the feast the remaining sweets were doled out among the families. A benevolent distributor rendered the sweet to a farmer from whose family nobody had turned up for desilting. He was surprised on their kind gesture. He quipped, "I had given rupees seven as my share and you are returning it in the form of sweets. Well, dig every week!"

12. The Drowning Factors

When you learn swimming it is possible enough that you come on the verge of drowning. In earlier times the ponds and canals used to be of irregular depths, you can say these were unfathomable at some places. The digging of ponds was unplanned and it was done as a community service voluntarily. Each family in the village contributed in this work and it was accomplished in the sweltering months of summer, just before the rainy season, so that sufficient amount of water might be collected in the pond. This sort of pond digging was done vigorously and with zeal, everyone aspired to include himself in this pious task, consequently its depth became inconsistent at several places. Due to heavy rains, the pool became overfilled and turned into risky watershed for the debut swimming. I myself nearly drowned not once but thrice.

I started my swimming practices in the neighbouring pond where we took the buffaloes for quenching their thirst. In summer these buffaloes generally reached the deepest place to cool themselves, piercing the water body. We also plunged into it simultaneously for adventure sake and also to scratch the buffaloes' back, to wash them properly. Buffalo's tail was helpful enough while practising swimming, we kept it captured to save ourselves from drowning and simultaneously flapped our arms and legs. Such used to be our initial steps of swimming. After some time we left the tails and started our apprenticeship on our own but there remained senior swimmers to look on. Yet swimming was never risk free.

The children play games in water, not like that of water polo. There in the pond, one of them challenges others to touch his head and they pursue him. When it is a game, the kids who are not swimmers also join them and here evolves the risk of drowning. I was also a fledgling in swimming and trying myself in the shallow water, but inadvertently I once, flapped with the flock who were running after the challenging boy. The water was getting deeper and myself indecisive, before I knew anything, I felt sinking. Whatever I had learnt about swimming, was slipping from my mind. I got panicky, gulped water, flapped indiscriminately and frantically. The boys sensed the situation and one struck me with a head push. I was frightened badly, took the shore unconsciously.

13. Crossing a Canal

Swimming in a canal along the banks is one thing and crossing it, is another. Initially I started my swimming practices in ponds of uneven depths where the water is still and learning in standstill water is dissimilar to learning in flowing water. Then I marched towards the canal which flowed at a distance of half kilometers from our village. The canal banks were not refined as these are today, reeds and weeds thrived there and wherever these were not growing, the canal guards restore them by fixing the thorny shrubs for protection of shores from the animals. The thicket-forming bushes nurture dangerous creatures like snakes and it was horrifying to go near them.

My age might be eleven or twelve years. After the school closing at one pm, numerous boys used to rush towards the canal to dive to cool them in scorching summer. I remember, I hurriedly tossed out my school bag in the house and ran with other children, with expectations of learning swimming. Due to scorching heat we flung ourselves in water speedily. But I kept myself along the banks safely; of course I became a moderate swimmer in a few days. But you are not a fair swimmer until you learn crossing the canal. My skilled friends cajoled me several times to take the step of crossing, but I trembled to think so and went on procrastinating for several days.

One day the boys prepared me and they promised their full support, would not let me drown in the middle. So, we all a flock of six or seven boys flung in tandem from the bank of the canal, I in the middle of the team was flapping legs and arms in water, eyeing on the other shore, kept advancing. The companions also swam surrounding me, with caring and cajoling. But in midstream, I lost my courage and began going up and down, forgot swimming, nose and mouth started inhaling water, no shore in sight, anticipated the imminent end. The boys caught me, dragged me to the other side of canal. Anyhow they were successful in saving me from sinking; I recollected courage after a long time to go near water.

14. Learning Cycling

Learning cycling has ever been fascinating and also adventurous. I learned it on bicycles of standard size. Of course it is convenient to debut on a mini cycle or even a lady cycle due to its curved top pipe which is easier to ride cross legged. But such sizes of protracted categories were rarely available at that time. If someone chanced to get a bicycle in our troupe, everybody got a trial more or less. It was impossible to ride cross legged on a standard sized bicycle, so we tried it in a scissors position, just approaching the other side pedal under the top pipe. I apprenticed in cycling after numerous and regular trials. Bumping, falling and getting injuries became routine. Sometimes our teacher gave us his bicycle to be taken in the village to have a puncture fixed. We gladly dragged it to the puncture vendor and after the repair we took our time to practice turn by turn. There are no stipulated rules of learning such things like cycling and swimming, you have to expertise yourself on your own in these arts.

I recall three or four children ran behind me supporting the carrier and I tried to balance it by pedaling in scissors position, intermittently they drew back to see me falling. That day an elderly boy, who was watching our practice, advised me, “If you want to learn cycling in one stroke then come up on this mound.” Considering him a wise person we laboriously reached at the top of the mound with the bicycle. He said, “you need not try in scissors position, be brave, come on the saddle straightway.”

I agreed and took a position on the saddle, that boy caught the carrier in still state, others around him. Then suddenly he detached himself, leaving me and the bicycle rolling down the steep slope. I found myself falling, and the bicycle upside down, leaving me bruised and hurt. Then I understood, "It is a folly to learn cycling in one stroke."

15. Summer Vacations

Everyone waited for the summer holidays which started from the last week of May. The teachers gave massive homework for the vacations keeping in view the number of days we would stay at home. We began to finish it day and night with efforts and strived to complete it in the first week of the vacations. Largely we accomplished it at the earliest, hoping to play without worries. Parents also kept on asking us about the conclusion of the vacation works, but virtually they had already predetermined the best use of our leisure time. During summer vacations I had to do the work of a herder, reason being our regular herding boy was engaged in other mainstream agricultural activities and the school going children like me were easy catch for rearing the buffaloes.

Pastures became expanses due to non-crop season of three to four months and hay gained time enough to grow self-sufficing and that season was a feasting season for the quadruped. After finishing vacations' homework, several of us, the scholars gave a helping hand to parents in such activities like raking the cotton plants, besides grazing the animals. We enjoyed in the meadows after assembling the flocks, because there was hardly any growing crop to poke in the open fields. I saw some herders were proficient enough in handling such domestic animals, by calling them with specific names and voicing some peculiar sounds, they made them to sit by such cajoling so that they might spare time to play and have pranks. In the last week of vacations the paddy plantation started, our task was diverted to supplying the tiny bundles of paddy saplings in the muddled field, where women planters were planting the saplings picking one by one. It was arduous enough to carry several bundles at a time, balancing yourself simultaneously on the raw silt fences. That was the most toiling work but was not taken in any consideration by anybody.

CHAPTER 4

16. Travesty of Justice

You may say it a travesty of Justice. I remember a court case from the neighbourhood. Two persons from the same village fought over an issue. From squabbling to man handling and then turned into a fiercely fight, one of them got injuries substantially. The victim approached the police station, the other one tried the patch up unsuccessfully and the case was registered. Then trial ensued, Date after date they both had to present themselves in court months after months. Several years passed, time heals everything, and there remained no enmity between them. Even they began to come to court on one bicycle for the trial dates but case didn't finish for many years. The trials in our courts run with a snail's pace. The Justice seekers got frustrated due to long wait for the final decision, no concept is there like the speedy trials. Generally people avoid going to courts, apprehending the outcome and expenditures involved with time consuming exercise. In the modern times transport is available at least to reach the court on the stipulated date; otherwise it was arduous enough to walk on feet the long distances in older times. Once an old man got fed up with the frequent trial dates for he had to walk nearly forty kilometres up and down. Eventually the timing for trial dates also fixed within short intervals, hardly a week time. The old man tired of his lengthy walks every week, On an occasion he got infuriated on listening the next date and shouted at the honourable magistrate, "what is this going on, date after date, how long will the trial run? I am fed up with the lengthy and tedious walking which I have to undergo week after week, I am ready even for conviction." The magistrate after listening his challenging arguments announced the judgment and awarded him five years imprisonment. The old man seemed relaxed on the conviction and said, "No regrets, I will endure it buoyantly." (saja ne hans ke katunga).

17. The Munshi of a Lawyer

'Justice delayed justice denied' This is rightly said about the judgments. Courts and counsels are taken fearsome by the common man. Reasons may be numerous. There is a long way to get any justice. The judicial system is cumbersome enough to go through, Gigantic sizes of rules, laws, by laws, sections, sub sections, paras, sub paras, appendices, provisions, amendments, there is unending series of terms and phenomena, enough for mind wriggling. Of course there are expertise of this field but expensive enough, beyond the affordability of the commoners. When it is advised to someone to consult a lawyer or go to court he thinks twice and generally backtracks. Whatever a lawyer claims about procuring justice in the beginning at the time of hiring; dives down with the passing of time. The lawyer no longer maintains a friendly demeanor with the client. Just getting dates after dates becomes the routine, pretexts and excuses come out more. With such treatments of the counsel, a common man finds himself hopeless and feels mired.

Longevity of the court cases dates after dates, hearing after hearing and appeals after appeals all have their contributions to make a lawsuit lifelong entanglement.

There is another significant cog noticeable enough in the judicial machinery, he is called 'munshi' lawyer's assistant who keeps on perturbing a client. Initially when the justice seeker comes to hire a lawyer the latter personally entertains him and elicits a handsome amount from him as his fee. The munshi remains tight lipped and the client doesn't foresee his role in the matter. But at later stages the munshi is pushed forward to attend the pitiable client. At every date the lawyer doesn't demand any more fee, but his assistant, the munshi doesn't exempt even a single occasion to get something out of him. I know a person who had to hire a counsel two or three times earlier, was victimized by the munshi frequently. But this time when he went to engage a lawyer he was circumspect enough. He said candidly, "this time I am hiring a lawyer only and not a munshi." (sirf vakil karunga munshi nahin).

18. The Diet and the Mind

How does the meal affect the functioning of your mind? What type of food enhances the efficiency of your thinking process? What should be the quantity of eatables to be taken that could sustain you as a smarter thinker? Such sorts of questions are often discussed. Their answers may be spotted by glancing at the people, their places they come from, their diet habits and also their achievements in respective arenas. If we see researches in science, the space engineering, medical science and also defence related explorations, most of the names that come forward are of those personalities who hail from South India. Rice is their staple food. They take sea food in their meals. And such types of cuisines are lighter and easily and early appetizing as compared to the foodstuffs of North Indians who have wheat as their main cereal. Another thing is that a person who does more physical works needs more calories in comparison with a white collar person.

These things are not new findings, and a layman often talks about them, it may be said that these are the tasted and experimented and also observed upon time. I know a person who is himself unlettered but a habitual litigant, remains connected to lawyers and counsels. He chooses such consultants with much shrewdness. In one of his lawsuits, his lawyer called him at noon at his house to discuss about the preparation for next hearing. When he reached the lawyer's home, what he sees that the lawyer is going to have his lunch, a larger platter on the table in front of him. The quantity of foodstuffs was as much as it should have been sufficient for three adults. The man cogitated for some time while the honourable lawyer devoured his platter absolutely. The impetuous gentleman immediately demanded his envelope of documents back, and said with assertion, "hefty meal will surely reduce your mental efficiency, my imprisonment is sure." (itna khha ke dimag ni chala karta).

19. The Study of Law

To do LL. B. has never been so arduous if anybody so aspires. Because, there are wide range of study materials. When one gets admission in first year, he is very much concerned about the classes, indulges in mutual discussions, and consults teachers for standard books. Initially one collects the books of illustrious authors and retains them every time in hand ostentatiously. Then after some time, he comes to know about the nutshells which attracts him and sets aside immediately the lengthy and weighty volumes. The seniors don't disclose about the uncomplicated and affordable study material in the beginning, for not being exposed earlier. Gradually everybody mingles with each other and mutual relations develop. Firstly, thirty questions series is revealed and they profusely recommend it by telling that it contains everything, you need not to read a voluminous one. Then comes the twenty questions series and later ten questions series. Now senior has no need to advise, the Junior has become proficient enough, he can seek the easy and accessible reading materials and also alternative ways to be successful in examinations without studying.

The Department of Law endeavors continuously for the better quality of education and learning, so that students adopt extensive reading. I remember, just before the examinations the pattern of question papers was proposed to be changed. In place of the criteria of attempt any five, another scheme in which one question from each five parts was proposed to be attempted by the examinees. The students got agitated, congregated and approached to the chairman's house at night by raising slogans against the new rules. The chairman was very upset to see such disruption and asked peevishly, "Is this a proper time to come my house, I don't want to talk with you." One of the students, who had taken admission in

Law after completing his physical education studies, spoke loudly, "Why would you not talk, you have to talk." (kyon ni talk, talk to karni padegi). The chairman perceived the gravity of the situation, and he dropped the idea of any reforms.

20. Incongruities of Dresses

Indian political persons particularly the congressmen put on khadi kurta pajamas with a cap, and they relate it to Mahatma Gandhi. I have never seen Gandhiji in such a dress. Dresses also make impression; an imprint of apparel goes in mind, particularly of the first encounter. Initially we come to know about far off states through their culture, their cultural dresses and we acquire such impression in our minds that the particular state always wears such costumes. If we have a look at the apparel of an Arunachal woman, it is too colorful with myriad patterns. Traditional costume of Assam is Mekhla Chaader, but many of these dresses are to preserve the customs and conventions. Mundum Neriyathum is the traditional dress of Kerala but that doesn't mean they wear it all the time, Kanchipuram Sarees are the fascination of a Tamil woman, but it is also donned on particular occasions. Punjabi doesn't wear the phulkari outfits every time or Haryanvi ladies don't take chunnar regularly. Even a number of these attires are related to various seasons and milieu also.

Most discernible getup is of an Indian lawyer he has to wear coat throughout the year, in all twelve months. Time and again this issue has been discussed by the bars. This custom of donning the coat came from Britain, a cool place and we followed it blindly. Even in May and June lawyers may be seen wearing a burden of coat. I remember once I asked a lawyer friend in the month of May, "Don't you feel sweltering heat in a coat." What he answered, it is also interesting. He said in his befitting tone, "If money comes continually, he is ready to wrap himself in a quilt." (Je pisse aate rah na haam to seod ki bukal bhi Mar layan)

21. Impractically Located Places

Extensive and prospective planning is lacking in the context of Indian towns and cities. As the population increases, a town expands itself in all directions; the more amenities have to be provided. Schools which were sufficient earlier, seem burdened with students, the hospital which was handling the erstwhile residents comfortably, is now appears overcrowded, and citizens seem dissatisfied with the treatment. The transport system is more haphazardly designed, even the main bus stand and the railway station which should be conjoining, are at antipodal locations. A person, who has traveled long in a train, will have to cover whole of the city to reach at the main bus stop to catch a bus. What is more conspicuous in the enlargement of a city is the slum boom which multiplies indiscreetly.

Numerous government offices which should be located nearer to each other are scattered throughout the city, tiring enough for people. Later came the concept of mini secretariat that houses a number of offices together, are also not constructed in every city. In spite of assimilation of numerous offices, several departments are working outside, wherever they were working earlier, due to unavailability of space. Even the police stations which should be strategically located in a city, so that immediate redressal of the law and order problems might be achieved, are situated at odd places. If displacement of such offices becomes essential, it should be done at easily accessible places.

I remember an incident from a town. Its main police station had been in the central part of the main market, near a renowned school. Due to congestion, a new and larger building was erected on the periphery of the town, near the canal. For some period two or three policemen remained posted at the older place. A man from a village came with some sort of grievance. The policemen apprised him the location of newly constructed police station. The man was astonished to listen about the new and far away located position of the police station. He quipped, "Is the new location practical." (itni door ke thana chal ja ga).

22. The Language Problem

How the accent confuses, syntax matters and diction impresses the listener. All these make difference between what is said and what is perceived. A police commissioner from South India gained popularity in Haryana due to his working style. Whichever district he served he was liked by the common man because he often listened grievances beyond stipulated hours, took new initiatives to apprehend the hardships people confront. He activated the entire department and tried to resolve problems faced by the public. Being a South Indian he had a weaker hand at Hindi and often ludicrous situations evolved. At that time he was posted at Karnal. One night he alighted from a train at the platform after completing his Delhi journey. The time was nearing twelve; he hired a rickshaw to reach his residence. He often does such things to know more about the citizens' problems. He enjoyed the conveyance, completed the distance with a vigilant look, as does a policeman.

Just after reaching his residence he called a sub inspector and ordered, "Go immediately and look near the railway station 'teka kuli hai'. The sub inspector didn't perceived the things clearly and haphazardly took a constable with him, reached the station and called all the coolies, asked them who Teka or Tekchand was, and what wrong he had done. He concluded that there was no coolie named Teka. He rushed back to report the commissioner that there was nobody named Teka. The commissioner lashed out at them, "I saw with my own eyes 'teka kuli hai'. The policemen dashed again to the railway station and searched thoroughly but got no clue about the 'teka kuli'. Now the time was nearing 2 am. They got frustrated, gulped some pegs from an open liquor vend and again reached to the commissioner to report about the futile raid. The commissioner was furious to see them drunk and shouted, "I was saying a liquor vend is open beyond scheduled time and it is clear now you both have drunk there on the 'Teka Khuli', (open liquor vend). Now go and face the action in the morning.

CHAPTER 5

23. Political Boasting

It is said that most of the leadership develops in student life. The boys, who begin politics while studying, become the leaders of tomorrow. What I observe a majority of student leaders don't have anything to do with studies, even they are instrumental in deviating others from learning. They start to achieve their aim by socializing and even by frolicking. In general they advance in their long cherished plan and it is ironical that such people who don't have any vision lead the government later. What can be expected from a person whose target have been just to do politics. They apply every ploy which is effective in the attainment of their goal and often indulge in sectarian politics of casteism, religion, regional favouritism and do everything except development. This thing is the root cause of our sluggish development. We have not reached where should have been.

Boasting and bragging are common in politics. Who starts doing politics, attains the title of pradhan at the earliest. The pradhan makes himself accustomed with gags and brags. By boasting he tries to impress his companions and in different degrees he succeeds. This practice is started at the earliest even in student politics. While studying I observed a pradhan was impressive enough and seemingly powerful. Whichever department he visited, the chairperson greeted him with all courtesies.

Not only pradhan but his companions also like me got good receptions. Then, It was time of legislative elections. I and pradhan were visiting Delhi with someone, a ticket seeker. On way back, we halted at Murthal for some refreshment. It was night time. The pradhan proposed to have beer and the next moment we were holding beer bottles in our hands and enjoying it sip by sip on the highway. I didn't feel fear of law due to pradhan. Soon what I saw a police Gypsy stopped, five or six cops started capturing the offenders who were drinking standing on the open road. The inspector put his hands around our necks. I saw towards the pradhan, who hurriedly freed his neck and rushed towards our vehicle across the road, I also followed him jerking my neck instantly. That day I realized that the pradhan was not powerful enough; and also not above law.

24. Waning of Popularity

A journalist once congratulated British Prime Minister Winston Churchill on organizing a highly successful rally in London. Churchill thanked him and also added, "More people will congregate if I am hanged there." I am citing this fact because nobody knows when public alters its mind and popularity becomes naught. I have witnessed the leaders crying for votes, who had been highly preferred persons in fair weather. Once a politician had to enact a drama by thrusting himself in a village pond, threatening to commit suicide, to get a promise for votes from the rural folks, but on the day of counting of votes, he was nowhere in fight. Another leader once of the same stature, got his popularity dwindled with the passing of time, and was unable to have respectable franchises in successive elections. Lately he was seen blubbering to the substantially gathered crowd, “A king cobra is not waiting for you under my election symbol, why don’t you press it?”

It is time which changes and charisma fades. Of course new leadership emerges and it becomes difficult to survive in politics with new generation, once they go off road politically. Another eminent figure in politics whose popularity was talk of the time in an era, struggled even to campaign peacefully, people often ridiculed him and it became arduous for him to address. In a village he had to address his last public meeting at night. He had not anticipated such trouble people would create. He faced continuous hooting in that village, notorious for such activities. It was dark enough; he got dust hurling and the urchins surrounded and pinched him. His companions came to rescue and asked what was happening. He said in a squally voice, “they were demanding badges.” (bille mange thhe, bille).

25. Politicians and Jobs

Entertainment is found profusely in politics. The propaganda of ruling party politicians mainly focuses on facilities provided by them to the common man. They will elaborate how much the present government has spent on education, on medical facilities, on providing better transport system. They have upgraded the irrigation techniques, the overall infrastructure. They are trying to uplift living standard of the poor. But people are least interested in these announcements and continually hanger on them for their personal causes and often show their indifference towards the common causes. If people are not getting personal work done, the leaders become the laughing stock. Public embark upon derision. The main motive of everybody is capturing government job.

The people exhibit their affinity, their closeness with the leaders by adorning them with currency notes garlands and invite them at their homes for feasts and banquets. I have myself witnessed such spectacles many times. Once a person invited a legislator at his house and entertained him with all possible means. He was handing over the cup to the honourable guest and asking simultaneously, "Is it certain that my son will be selected." (chhora laig bhi jaiga).

At other time during elections a man who invited a candidate for lunch, just to show his solidarity, introduced his two unemployed sons to the leader saying, 'these two should get government jobs'. (ye dono lanne hain). At another instance a set of six brothers were complaining to a veteran politician, "We are garlanding you in every election with currency notes chaplets but you have not employed even one of us. The leader then asked them, "Is anyone of you educationally qualified for a government job). What the elder of the six brothers retorted, "No one of them has ever gone to school." (pad rya ek ni).

26. A Political Rally

When a political rally is organized, the organizers may be seen at tenterhooks, worrying for the success of it. They make preparations several days earlier by holding meetings at different places, requesting people to reach, arrange for their transportation from their homes to rally place, assign duties to prominent workers for arranging drinking water for the gathering, their sitting arrangement, proper regulation of the traffic. The main leader takes his time to arrive at the raised pedestal and public feel discomfiture while waiting for a long period, an entertaining arrangement is also done, popular singers and clowns are invited and they keep the assemblage together. The rally of a political party is a sort of festivity for most of the workers and they enjoy their day fully in eating, gossiping and getting amusement.

The people are collected by the ticket aspirants; they reach at the rally ground sloganeering, by thumping drums, raising banners of their representatives, organizers. They throng at the green mattresses flattened for that purpose and continue sloganeering by standing in between the speeches. Sometimes there starts a competition among the slogan raisers. It is also an occasion of interception of old friends, acquaintances. Around the gathering a number of rahriwalas flock at certain gaps, selling the eatables like groundnuts warmed by an earthen pot emitting smoke, the cucumbers with vertical split and water being sprinkled intermittently. These eatables always lure the speech listeners. On one side of the gathering an enthusiastic worker whom people were calling pradhan gathered a considerable number of listeners around him by his gags, brags and fables. He continued impressing people by mentioning his close affinity with the top leadership and how much his roll matters in party affairs. A Pradhan's close associate who was feeling bored by his stories interrupted him all of a sudden saying, "you boasted enough, order for the salt sprinkled cucumbers." (batan bahot pel li ib kankarian ke nun luvale).

27. Agitation for Prohibition

He fought mainly for the farming community; he raised issues which were directly related to the agrarians. He fought for the better irrigation system, for releasing more canal water, for regular repair of the water channels, for regular supply of electricity for motor pumps so that crops might not dried up and ruined. He often raised voice against the sellers of spurious seeds, suppliers of ineffective and bogus pesticides. He agitated against the corrupt officials who regularly scuttled the government plans for the farmers' upliftment, who pilfered the funds assigned for cultivators, so that they could buy agricultural machinery, fertilizers on subsidised costs. He was known for his effective speeches, offbeat rhetorics and peculiar slogans. Once there was created a contrived scarcity of diesel, the government implemented rationing on fuel. The petrol pump owners took it as an opportunity to make profit; they compelled farmers to buy mobile oil with the diesel drums. The gentleman unified the milk suppliers, made them agreed to sell the milk to those city dwellers who were ready to buy the cow dung simultaneously.

In later years he appended other issues like the dowry system, child education and other social evils. Once in a gathering, he suddenly started speaking on prohibition and said that the liquor consumption had increased manifold and it was devastating the families.

He also added that the boozers should be ostracized and disowned by the society. There was a young man in the gathering sitting near the pedestal, who used to procure him the aqua vitae, he was surprised to listen from the speaker such exhortations against drinking, stood up and objected, “uncle you are also a daily drinker”. Everyone was flabbergasted. The uncle browbeat him and retorted, “sit down, that is why I didn’t have golden fences.” (mere konse sone ke mundere oge).

CHAPTER 6

28. A Used Car

If you purchase an old vehicle, you develop close relations with a mechanic; he becomes your special friend. Even you start exchanging marriage and other ceremonies' cards with the 'friend in need' I observed this years back, when I bought a car, Maruti 800. Contrary to my earlier conception, I comprehended soon that single mechanic is not sufficient to maintain that oldie. A plethora of doers is required to keep that car pliable. I was acquainted with a series of working class, an engine mechanic, a battery mechanic, an interior carer, a music system repairer, a dent mender, a painter and also a puncture fixer. Of course some remain to be mentioned like bumperwala etc. Main problem I faced with that car was the starting problem, particularly in the morning. Often I had to request the ongoing people in street for a push start. When it failed after many trials the pushers had a peevish look towards me while leaving. I had to call the battery mechanic alternatively whom I visited at regular intervals.

I remembered the trick of the tractor starting in villages. What they used to do was that they didn't stop the engine in a general way, but they emitted enough smoke through the silencer by pressing the accelerator vigorously for some time, in order to keep the engine warmer for a prolonged duration. I tried it once likewise, before stopping the engine I pressed the accelerator more, the car made high din and emitted more smoke, then pressed more, eventually, the clutch slipped from under my foot, the bonnet of the car stroke at the staircases with a thud, got another dent. My son was clapping from inside the door.

29. The Blabbermouth

There are four categories of people in this world. First, there are wise and active fellows, they are of constructive nature and lead the people. In the second category comes unwise and inactive people, they know less and are doing no harm to anybody and that is why they are placed in the second category. In the third classification falls such people which are wise but inactive, they are not giving their due to the world. In the last comes the unwise but active and they might prove destructive. A prattler also comes in the last bracket. A Prattler is a person who talks a lot on a topic but knows nothing about that topic. Such people will intrude whatever the discussion may be. They just feel discomfiture if they have to remain silent for a period. Even they drag an earnest issue to meaningless, because proficient players retreat themselves from the debate, due to these childish fellows and their flimsy arguments. At many occasions they start gibbering without caring for the occasion and who is the listener.

Once my school going son had to attend a guest; a distant relative form a village. I was coming home in the afternoon, so the guest; a talkative fellow had to pass time with the boy. The boy continued listening to his bucolic issues without grasping all the things. The man went on elaborating the cost of chemical fertilizers, the hefty electricity bills, the labour problems etc. Everything flew over the head of the boy. But the guest carried on the talks of his interest and whatever he knew, like he sold his agricultural produces at that rate, two buffaloes at that rate, and an ox at that rate. He left the boy in utter confusion, because he had never confronted such blabber mouthed persons. In the evening after the departure of the guest the boy said to me, "why he was telling me all the things and I tell you dad, he had sold many things".

30. The Helping Hand

It is not bad to co-operate your life partner in kitchen work or other housekeeping tasks. If you do so, you will surely save her from the drudgery and monotonous tasks of three times cooking, brooming, and mopping and other routine exercises. Such unchangeable cycles affect the attitude and often lead to abnormal unfriendly behaviour of the doers. Even least assistance also matters and all such reciprocities create a harmonious atmosphere in a household. You will certainly be responsible for the smiles which reflect on doing a work cumulatively. But fastidious attitude hamper to garner mutual cooperation and joint exercises. Another thing is that sometimes such assignments are handed over to the other partner where more shrewdness and attention is required and in case of failures you might be admonished and mutual cooperation receive a massive blow in those circumstances.

Waiting for the milk emerging out of the pot until it starts evaporating and boiling, is very tiring and hardly gives you time to turn off the snap switch. Every time it takes different period in approaching towards the brims of the pot. I have to stand with stark attention watching below the tongs supporting the lid. My mind should not deviate in researching additional parts like the jet flamers, pilot tube, vent pipe or main valve and it will surely spill out if I think to steal some moments for newspaper reading. It is arduous enough to stand still and intermittently bending myself to see below the half closed lid. Warnings continue to shower down from the spouse who flits around like a darting mouse outside the kitchen, "you would certainly boil the milk out on slab and multiply my morning chores." And suddenly I see the entire body of milk start rising with a hissing sound like the floods of water from a dam; hurriedly I turn off the snap switch to keep it within bounds. Ah it is great relief !

31. The Conventional Clinics

There are fewer doctors who attend the patient directly. Generally, the modern clinics have been upgraded with posh waiting rooms where an LED display is hanging for entertainment. There are several staffers who perform multifarious duties in different cabins. You will be attended at the counter where your name, age and address are recorded and a smart consultation fee is to be paid. Then you have to wait for your turn to see the doctor who sits in a closed door cabin. He may recommend for some tests which are generally done inside the clinic in a different cabin. The doctor prescribes costly medicines which are available only at the shop located in the clinic. But conventional clinics are relevant as well as practical enough to treat people at lesser costs and in a better way.

It is always easy to be medicated from a regular and familiar doctor. You need not to tell every time your name, unwellness details and also what affects your organic structure. Most of the malady he perceives on seeing your face. The doctor I visit never inquires me much more and largely he is a man of taciturn nature. He just calls me to the revolving steel stool by insinuating. He presses the chest piece of his stethoscope here and there on my body and turns to the subscription pad uttering, "it is infection". He hands over the subscription slip to the boy in the cabin through a quadrilateral slot. I took my seat on the waiting benches, transfixing my eyes on Chhota an attendant, through the glasses of cabin, anticipating it should not be an injection. To my dismay Chhota comes out of the cabin brandishing a needle and approaching towards me. I entreat him, "look Chhota there shouldn't be pain, use the thinnest needle." I also ask him what is in the syringe. He tells, "nothing but vitamins." I again question him, "which vitamins?" While injecting and making me a little shriek he tells, "All vitamins in little quantities" (thhode thhode sarre hain).

32. To Whom You Yield

What quantum of amount should be given to the children for their routine expenses? As long as they live with you, particularly during schooling, you yourself manage the costs of every sort that include school fee, spending's on dresses, expenses on birthday treats and daily pocket money. The kids are within your preview twenty four hours, and even the company they entertain may be watched. But when your children cross the school education, join institutions at a distant city for higher education, your expenses suddenly increase many fold. The smaller amount which you were spending with cost effectiveness snowballs into substantially bigger, besides your young ones have to learn to handle hefty charges. Within months your concerns not only fade but your worries start, particularly in the cases of boys. He stops receiving advice and even starts to advise you on spending matters. He often mentions such brands of dresses which were not in vogue in your time.

Of course you happily part with the money, but your estimates are often betrayed. Your recommended brands, be it the matter of bike, mobile sets or the clothings, become defunct for him. You give him enough, even more than that your sources allow, but generally he remains demanding and more you offer, more his expenses grow. Sometimes you give an amount for a specific purpose; the boy consumes it on another unnecessary buying. I recollect some instances of my own. I once gave my son a considerable amount of money for the garments which he had asked for. A week passed but no new dress was noticed upon him. I enquired about the sum that was rendered to him. The youngster replied that he had spent the amount in organizing a friendly treat. I assumed the sum squandered. I recounted him the two lines of Faiz Ahmad Faiz, "Tormentor, you use your skill, shoot an arrow I offer my chest." (aa sitamgar tu apna huner aajma, mein seena aajmata hun to teer aajma).

33. The Voluble Guy

Oratory is an art. Many people have touched the sky by mastering it. A good orator would certainly shine. He will flow the words in a guarded way, like the water streams in a water channel, a soothing current without overflowing. A rhetorician is able to hold the crowd spellbound. There are two categories of speechmakers, one who makes the listeners understand in lesser words and the other who gives a lengthy lecture full of verbosity, goes on elaborating extensively. But that doesn't mean he gets lesser acclamations. Such types of orators are also effectual at many occasions. There is a person; I think he is from Public Relations Department, who falls into the second category. He is required when the speakers are in insufficient numbers and the time is enough.

Generally it is habit of leaders to reach late, reason may be several public meetings and prior engagements, there needed such a speechifier like the above mentioned fellow. Once upon a time I was a listener in such a public meeting. The organizer spoke first and then the other speakers one by one and soon there was a dearth of speakers. He, the voluble person held the mike, started speaking in his impressive clinking voice. he went on speaking, touching every issue, problems faced by different segments of the society, the environmental topics, from the municipality level issues to the global level. using verbosity, weighty and lighter words simultaneously. It is said about him that he can lecture even for twenty four hours. There was no respite, the man went on speaking. Then a listener who was sitting on a chair adjoining mine asked, "What is the name of this leader?" I told him, "Brother, this is not a leader, this is a radio."

CHAPTER 7

34. Treading the Passageway

He was not from our class but used to go across the gallery regularly, particularly during tea break, halting briefly at the gate of our class room, riveting his eyes to detect someone, then with a sudden turn marched forward on his way. He was a senior fellow with a peculiar personality, bearing a beard something like Chhatrapati Shivaji but neatly cropped, with a different makeover. He was highly impressed by the famous thespian Rajkumar, the Jani, wore dresses like him, in summer, spotless white safari suit with white shoes. Not only that but he proficiently imitated to have a gait like him, protruding the right arm obliquely while walking. In winter he always fixed a red rose on the ticket pocket of his coat, just like Jawaher Lal Nehru. He never missed the premiere show of his most cherished hero. He even traveled hundred kilometers to watch his movies.

But his treading the passage was significant enough. I don't remember he ever dropped his stroll through the passage, emerging out from a corner at the stipulated time when the bell rang for the short break; it was said about his fixed round that you could correct time on your wristwatch on his appearance in the passageway. Many of us didn't know the motive of his routine walking there, halting at the gate, exploring someone with curiosity, and then striding again in the corridor. That day also he arrived on the fixed time, stopped like earlier but his eyes were searching the familiar one but to no avail, some sort of disquiet feeling was spotted on his face, he then turned to leave, walked some steps but came back again on the door, everyone's eye on him, brooding on his sudden return. The guy announced to the class all of a sudden, "listen everybody, tell your friend, I had come, remember (keh dena apni saheli se hum aaye thhe)." Then again the gentleman proceeded ahead abruptly.

35. The Numberdar

You meet a person of limited material, you can enlist the things he convey every time repeatedly, these can be counted on fingers, even the impending commas and full stops can be speculated, still you entertain him and reciprocally you are also entertained. It is quite probable, either the person is a good articulator or his narratives are special and superb and can be listened and afforded repeatedly. But variations and newness have always been greatly required; these things are relatively valued more and listened with interest. Numberdar, as he preferred to be addressed, due to his ancestral status, is such a personality, who whenever meets me, provides fresh, impressive and thought provoking accounts and stories, of course concerning him and his acquaintances, largely he involves himself nearly in every episode. I asked him once about his neatly maintained car that seemed to be regularly washed. He told me in detail how his earlier vehicle gave in from the bottom due to his regular washing habit and also added that it was harmful, metal got rusted, but he was doing it for he had his own garage and service station both.

Gossips continued, in between I asked him about a particular friend of him, but he told me that they were estranged presently. I wanted to know the developments that led to their estrangement. He narrated me the whole story which is interesting enough. Once, the friend, of course estranged now, invited the Numberdar to his new establishment, perhaps an agency of some sort which he had opened a few days earlier. On perpetual requests Numberdar went to his establishment, asked about his friend, the owner and his cabin office and someone pointed towards the direction. As he walked to the cabin office, a uniformed attendant intercepted him. The attendant apprised him about the order of the boss that he had to wait for twenty minutes to see him. At this the Numberdar got infuriated, turned instantly and departed by saying, "Gentleman, "I will meet your boss when he comes on the road." (jab tera malik sadak per aa jayega tab mil lunga).

36. The Insolent Boy

He did nothing except mischiefs and that up to the level of devilry. In college he was notorious for frolicking. In the bicycle stand he often deflated the cycle tyres to perturb the students, kicked one of the cycles to see the falling all in line, the cycles got jumbled, laying on each other. The boys had to struggle to detach their wheels. He went to library only to disturb the serious readers by slow whistling, mewing or by other mimicking sounds. He often made the juniors frightened by placing the replicas of spiders and mice on their books unexpectedly. He came in the college on a motorbike which used to be without silencer and its din could be imagined, that blaring stringent noise was sufficient to trouble the tranquil atmosphere of the educational institution. In the classroom also he was a nuisance for the teachers; it was difficult enough to keep the concentration on teaching and many a times he was reprimanded for his roguishness. The teachers had to tell him to go out of the class and complained to the principal about his rascalities.

The principal often called him, advised him to be good, and even warned him against his daily heightening misdoings, but all efforts by the college staff proved waste. Sometimes he with his likeminded friends often stood in the entrance to make the girl students embarrassed and chagrined. One day he sat on the carrier of a bicycle while a girl was riding it. Due to his mischief the girl fell on the ground with her bicycle and got bruised and injured. The principal was informed about the occurrence. The principal called the boy's grandfather who was a reputed politician of the region. The boy was also called in the office. After listening to all the complaints; the grandfather stood from his seat and started thrashing him and dragged him out, among the students and again beat him with shoes. After the incident, his friends gathered around him and said, "you knew your grandpa's nature, you shouldn't have gone near him, inadvertently you got insulted." But the insolent boy uttered, "Insult is immaterial, it would have been a problem if grandpa stopped giving money."

37. The Comrade

He had come to study law from a small village of western Haryana. He was a social fellow with a smiling face supporting a thin beard. He often discussed current affairs, fond of newspapers reading, a sincere reader of editorials, remained updated and aware as a pleasing person in the company. He came into contact with a student wing that supported socialism and talked of equal opportunities, equal distribution of sources and wealth. Soon he attracted towards them, due to their appealing principles, where dreams might be realized. He immersed into the outfit naturally with a watchable fervour and adopted the wardrobe of a common man, a kurta pajama, the kurta loose and long enough hanging up to the knees. He kept a special bag with long string like a 'bijyoti' (seed bag), slinging from his shoulder. I don't know what he used to keep in the special satchel but it is certain there might have been magazines of some sort, particularly Russian literature.

They held meetings every week and made efforts to increase their strength and more or less they succeeded in their endeavors. I also observed about them that they never discussed their agenda at the canteen assemblages. They made contacts with new students individually at their rooms and offered membership of their unit; They gave them a slip after receiving membership fee of a few rupees. Meanwhile the guy got selected in some subordinate service in Delhi. His companions often requested him to spare time for weekly meetings. He came once on sabbatical and sojourned with his older companions. He attended the meeting but it was conspicuous enough that his older zeal had gone. He was least interested in theoretical talks of equality and socialism. He was cajoled to speak something. Anyhow he spoke in the end, "friends, I have wandered enough, there is no scope of any socialism anywhere, and engage yourself in your work." (apna apna dhandha dekh lyo). The meeting ended in a hilarious tone.

38. A Name does Matter

Some names are so catchy and soothing; they attract the attention of others per se. I am talking of Gullu, who will surely pardon me. The guy was very popular, not just because of his name, but for the activities he generally used to do. He bore a smiley round face on a substantially plump body, absolutely doing justice with his name. Among the skinny fellows he was comparatively healthier and chubbier. At that time he often talked about the ways of getting slim, like taking a lemon every morning, empty stomach. These things surprised us in those days due to our already skinny figures. He always held authority at gatherings, especially at canteen and common entertainment room, with his hilarious talks and pranks. Everyone felt comfortable in his company.

Although he was of urban upbringing, yet he was equally popular in ruralites, and always listened the folk songs and ragnis. he had a great perception about folklores and popular singers of that time, and always stored a good collection of such songs. Virtually he was a votary of local culture and customs. How he, a product of public schools, inclined towards ragnis, particularly 'competition music' is beyond my comprehension. But that doesn't mean he was restricted to it, he was versatile, and took interest in every interesting arena. In stadium when games were held, Gullu attracted much attention than the players, with his special catchy slogans and piercing voice. His room generally remained full with friends and visitors. In spite of his social engagements, he was never lacking in studies, nobody knew when he did his preparations. Once he shifted his room on another floor. The boy who occupied Gullu's earlier room had to write on the door, "Gullu left this room' (Yahan Gullu nahin rahata).

39. The Examinations

University auditorium was a hub for new and popular movies particularly in examination days. It had been a matter of deliberations, why the movies were shown in precious time for examination preparations, but in the minds of university authorities, it would be a respite for the examinees whom they thought engrossed in books, to relieve them from the reading pressure. Besides auditorium there were several things for amusement. Students passed their time watching serials, matches and movies in television at the recreational room. Carom board was also there for indulging in mutual competitions. Volleyball net was also erected in hostel where students played matches throughout the day and made considerable cacophony constantly and disturbing the seriously studying students. Many of them had least time for study if we look at their hectic schedule of indulgence in student politics and gossiping. But I discovered that students in majority never kept stress nearby even looked more delighting and entertaining in examination seasons. Assemblage at canteen, chatter and natter, jokes and humour suddenly were on rise. Yet students remained conscious enough about the speedy preparations.

They tried detours for this purpose like discussing with a bookish student and by this method they availed enough passing material. Another was preparing through nutshells to get the crux of syllabi. Above all were the impersonations and cheating. Friendship of the whole year was used in impersonating the exam by some more socializing guys. Cheating was the most prevalent way to pass the papers. The instances of rusticity were also there. A student was caught using unfair material in examination. The invigilator readied the unfair means case. The supervisor nudged him to apologize to the invigilator for his wrong doing. The impudent student just said, "pardon, pardon." The invigilator admonished him, "You don't know even how to apologize." On this the rude boy retorted," I am not going to tether a buffalo in your house." (aur tera mes band ke aun) Thus he got the Unfair Means Case confirmed.

40. The Boarding Boy

Listening to him speaking is very soothing. It is usually said about some people. Have you ever contemplated upon it? One thing is that if someone is such a speaker who articulates the things without obscurity and sounds both ends of a word, listening and comprehending the spoken substance becomes comfortable. In other way, let's understand it, he is not devouring the half word and divulging the other half. Another significant thing I observe is the usage of the words which abound in solid and sound syllables like t and p. Additionally, dodging the nasal sound words, also makes the communication soothing and attractive. Urdu language is a fine example of the above where we hear minimum nasal sounds comparatively. But the person, who has treasure of words in Hindi, of course in any mother tongue, is staggeringly superb. In any companionship such orator would certainly be appealing and enthralling.

I am talking about one of my classmate, who had a brilliant word strength and ability of their timely applications, be it Hindi or English. He was a boarding breed, completed his school education from various states, for his parentages were military personnel and that made him a different personage. While speaking he captivated people with word clarity and rich vocabulary along with his joviality. He often stole the show at the canteen assemblages or at the retiring room. He had a number of stories about the places he stayed earlier, like boarding pranks, about the military personnel, his own experiences and expeditions. He even elaborated the material gathered during the day in an entertaining style. His company was really invigorating for being a good humoured guy. He was witty enough. It was a discussion about admission seats in M.Phil. A boy, who had studied in a village up to secondary level, was claiming his admission on rural seat. At this the boarding breed retorted, "You simply look rural, you need not to show any document." (tu to yar lagta hi rural hai).

CHAPTER 8

41. Greeting of a Love Letter

Dormitories were famous for congregations, assemblages and throng of the students. Study remained there as a second priority. There were always laughter, amusement and giggling whenever friends gathered, energized themselves, some of them with trivial talks. That day a younger student who mixed easily and early with the seniors, was taking views of others upon the matter of letter writing. As we know there are five parts of a letter like the heading, the greeting, the main text called body, the complimentary closing and the signature. He had to write a perfect wooing letter to his desired and cherished sweetheart. He said he had prepared the main body of the letter and he wanted a beautiful, special and captivating greeting to start with. So many words and proposals were offered by the companions. One of them said he should start with dear, but it was declined due to its commonness. Another proposed darling, but it was also rejected with the same reasons.

An English literature student forwarded the word 'my treasure', for his greeting address. It was also denied on the basis of wealthy considerations. 'My honey' was also pushed forward by the same literature person, but this greeting was too rejected due to its sticky properties. A Sanskrit studying boy told him that he should use lighter and softer words for his greeting like 'priye', This was also not agreed upon by the stylish young man, saying it was too much conventional and old fashioned. Then entered Mr. Malik; a burly boy with a clinking voice. Everybody looked towards him, and one of them told him about the debate issue, and also about the words that were offered for the greeting of a love letter and also about the continuous rejections by young man. At this Mr. Malik said vibrantly, "This is not a big issue, I have written dozens of such letters, and if you are not agreeing on these greetings offered by friends, then you should just write 'Reverend mother, I touch your feet' right!" (pujye mataji charan spursh). Everyone was swooning with laughter.

42. Milk Pilferage

I recall another dormitory scene. This dormitory was on the ground floor in the opposite block of mine just near the walkway. Canteen surrounded by lawns was in the midway of both the blocks. The dormitory was occupied by some sportspersons perhaps wrestlers fully carefree fellows. They seldom lock their dorm and strange guests visited them frequently particularly in those days when there was any tournament, youth festival or any cultural carnival. These dorm room residents were also active in students' politics and that thing too multiplied their guest number. These sorts of rooms are generally allotted to two students but there always lived more than the requisites. They might be seen doing exercises sometimes outside the big room. But generally they left for the stadium at 5.00 in the morning.

A milkman supplied them milk daily. But he visited the dormitory in absence of these wrestlers when they were on the playground. He just put the five litre can full of milk on table near the couches. After workouts, exercises and much perspiration they came after 8.00 am from the stadium with conviviality, humming the filmy songs. They enjoy the milk after heating, pouring it in one jug and then in another tumbler to make the temperature normal. One day what they found that the milk can was there but it was empty. They came out furiously, shouting 'who dared to drink their milk,' and even used abusive language for the culprit. Everybody was surprised to see what had happened to the grapplers. Then they turned towards the guest, a skinny, extra slim fellow who was staying overnight in the dormitory and still sleeping covering himself with a blanket. "Tell who drank our milk" And the guest replied submissively, "Manne batti si li thhi" (I had just taken a tablet). The wrestlers were glancing at the gangling physique of the guest and the five litres can alternatively.

43. The Cot Problem

The modern paying guest system is not so hospitable and congenial as it signifies, virtually these are wrongly connected terms, for where there is guest, how he can be a paying person, and he should be called a client. Even there is nothing like that of euphemism in this terminology, it is actually a misnomer which stands for nothingness. Generally the paying guest homes are highly congested and overcrowded places, thick air reigns there, you have to come out even to breathe comfortably. In a small cubicle, numerous students are lodged. Their overall motive is to spin money, to extract bucks from the dwellers. These are constructed with single purpose that how maximum numbers of persons can be stuffed into it, even the furniture which is placed in the room is specially prepared, everything slender and narrow, the table and chairs looked like toys.

Sometimes such hardships were also there in university but not up to the level of PG homes. Now and then a dormitory also became thronged. In spite of its larger size it was a crowded place, always full of commotion. Besides allotted students there lived casual students and frequent guests. Of course there remained dearth of cots. Everybody was not lucky enough to get a cot for sleeping and generally many of them straighten their bed near the gate on the floor, like a tailor in a cloth shop. They were generally seen imploring to get cot for one night. Once one of them was requesting earnestly," I will lay on the bamboo of the cot." (main khhat ki bai pe pada rahunga). The boy on the cot retorted, "Cling to the bamboo that is standing in the corner (jo kone mein lathh khhada hai, uske chipat jya)."

44. The Sluggish Students

In one of the dormitories there lived two students named Billu and another Tillu. Their friendly relationship was unparalleled and incomparable. Intimacies develop due to certain common traits, common likings, equal mental level, matching life style and above all homophonic nature. They were from the same class, doing post-graduation in History. and they comprehended each other in a few days and that resulted in sharing a common dormitory. Sooner other students also acknowledged the duo and their commonalities, their jocundity and jocularity. They were pleasing fellows, respectful and everyone experienced comfortability in their company.

But what were conspicuous about both of them, that I observed was their lethargic habits, they were slumberer and snoozer, enjoyed their long sleep generally. Many a time they skipped even their meals to avoid walking to the mess in a state of sluggishness and prefer to order for the room service. Once I visited their dormitory and what I saw, there was untouched meal, flies humming upon the platter, the thhali, both slumberous enough to bother for food. I just asked why they weren't taking food. Tillu replied yawningly, "We sacrificed it for the flies." I smiled and asked them, "Just tell me, what your hobbies are." One of them answered while gaping, "to listen slow pitched news on radio (dhimi gati ke smachar sun na)." I understood the height of lassitude.

I recall another instance from a different place. During student life students generally live sluggish life. In the rooms they keep everything scrambled. I lived in hostel and occasionally visited my friends who were living in a hired room in city. Once I visited them in afternoon. For courtesy sake they prepared tea for all. My friend announced that tea is ready and you just upturn the cups from the table and also take a likka (strong wooden spike) to scratch because these aren't cleaned for three days.

45. Sneaking Habits

Largely there were no thefts in hostels, the students were unconcerned about sneaking possibilities, and they locked their rooms only once, while going to classes.

In other circumstances, like going to the mess, during canteen sittings, gathering at porch or watching television even for a long time, they rarely bothered to lock. The transistor sets were got stolen of many students, and the thief was never apprehended. Petrol pilferage was prevalent enough even among some swanky fellows, who afforded motorbikes but pipes and empty bottles were noticeable in their rooms, they were doing it admittedly. Sumptuousness was also visible in a few guys, they spent their money extravagantly, but often became tight handed, and hefty canteen payments remained overdue towards them, due to their delinquencies. Many times they had to borrow from the less privileged students.

I remember a dormitory scene on my floor in the hostel. Three or four students lived in that dormitory, all jovial fellows. They regularly celebrated parties, two to three times within a week. Several students from other hostels frequently visited them. Whiskey, chicken, full music and dance remained the routine concept. They continued their jubilation and festivity till late night. In a cubicle, neighboring room, there lived an astute fellow. When the party was in full swing in dormitory, everybody inebriated, dancing to the tune, he sneaked in by opening the door cautiously. He mingled with dancing folks, making dancing poses and stealthily approached the chicken tub placed in a corner, picked a chicken leg, posturing with the dancing guys, came out of the room. He didn't miss the occasions and enjoyed free chicken several times. The pilferage was caught after a long time.

CHAPTER 9

46. Hobbyhorse

Music is inherent in human nature and generally there are no requirements of special instruments to draw it out. It may erupt anytime and anywhere. It might be seen people start singing while riding a bullock cart, while ploughing the field; women begin humming while fetching water from a distant well, with a considerable load of the earthen pot full of water on their heads, even while grinding the flour. But there is a tendency to polish, to embellish the music. People start using the snapping fingers, tapping a match box, even thumping a tin mug. Rama and Shyama, the two brothers were very fond of music. Euphony was in their veins. They produced symphonic sounds without any instrument. Whenever they found time from their daily chores like cutting the fodder and serving it in the manger, milking the buffaloes, they began buzzing the melodies. Whenever there were singing competitions, musical concerts, musical dramas, they listened them attentively and rehearsed for many days.

Then they planned to buy some sort of instrument to play and learn the music in a better way. After a few days they purchased a used one harmonium. Due to hectic cropping season, they hardly spared time to play it in daytime. Both started to rehearse after supper till late night. However they hadn't any formal training nonetheless they stepped to coherent playing. One tried his hand on the harmonium another sang with his sustained throaty voice with a great zeal. They were harnessing the instrument with continued practice and enjoying its melodies. One day a neighbour came to their house in the evening. He said that there were guests staying at his home and he required their harmonium. Rama and Shyama beamed to hear about the demand and gave the instrument uttering, "Do the guests harbor such hobby." The neighbour quipped, "It is not the matter of hobby, I want for them a tranquil atmosphere for a sound sleep, and your blare would disturb them."

47. The Terror of a Bank Jeep

The green revolution came as a boon for the agrarian community. The work began at many platforms. Due to new researches, a large increase in crop production was achieved. Technology was transferred to the farmers, new initiatives were undertaken. High yielding varieties of cereals were introduced, irrigation infrastructure was expanded to far off farms, management operations were modernized, and artificial fertilizers were also distributed along with hybrid seeds and pesticides. It is said that Norman Borlaug, the Nobel laureate saved mankind from starvation. Otherwise human being had to depend on the sea food. In India Dr. Swami Nathan is credited with the green revolution who changed the agricultural system in a big way.

Money was required to introduce the new techniques, government offered credit to farmers profusely. People made its use in uplifting the crop production as well as their own lifestyles. The amount of loans went on increasing manifold, the farmers began to face tough times in repaying the bank loans. The government adopted stringent laws to realize the distributed credits. There came a time when there was a great terror of bank jeeps. The farmers who took loans from banks and cooperative societies, sometimes failed to repay the annual installments, due to natural vagaries like flood, draught etc. The bank officials put the defaulters forcibly into their jeeps and confined them for a period, till the installment was realised.

Virtually it was a cruel practice on the part of the bank officials. It was a matter of disgrace for a farmer if any such vehicle halted in front of his house. Even no one took a lift from a bank jeep. Once the bank officials reached a farmer at his farm to demand the money. The farmer told them that he had paid the installment the day before. Inadvertently, the officials had no perception about the yesterday's payments. They said to the farmer if it was true, then the receipt slip should be produced. He apprised them that the slip was at home. The officials offered him lift to his house. The farmer declined the lift saying if he had to sit in a bank jeep, then there was no need to deposit the installment. He came to his house on foot walking along the jeep, of course keeping some distance.

48. The Voracious Fellow

He practiced wrestling from the early age, when he was a herder. There was a pattern of things at that time, buffaloes kept there in the peripheral common land for a long time, before being carried to the pastures. They stayed there in flocks, chewing the cud, and a drover didn't need to care more for the quadruped and thus got enough time for entertainment. He turned to grappling during this leisure time and soon he was able to flatten several fellow herders of his age. In a few days he was popular in the game throughout the village. Athletics and wrestling competitions were held on the occasions of festivals, and he always proved himself as a champion. Forthwith he stepped ahead and began participating in fights in neighbouring villages and there also he didn't look back, fully utilized his burly physique. In those days a wrestler used to receive full exposure at the fairs organized annually, people in large numbers assembled in these carnivals. Wrestling remained there main attraction. People enjoyed several bouts there, watched the grappler circulating in the ring, thumping his thigh, symbolizing an open challenge. His challenge was peculiar and the spectators held their breath to see who would come forward to the formidable fight. His bout filled the crowd with full excitement, by applying his full force he made his opponent collapsed and celebration ensued.

He never attended a school, his main occupation remained herding, his repast was also enormous, gulped too much, it was even said about him that he was a voracious fellow. At the meadows he asked for the churma, a popular cuisine from the ongoing women. If someone abjured in rendering him the churma, he acquired it even forcibly. One day a woman who was coming from her relations foresaw the expected swipe, she pretendedly told him that she belonged to a

lower caste. But such concepts were immaterial for the ravenous guy. He took the churma uttering, "he had snatched such grub from a woman of higher caste, I will blend both to make it similar to that of a middle caste.

49. The Wise Old Man

It is said that the whole family can not watch the television program together due to semi vulgar scenes telecast. Even ads are not far behind in creating such nuisances. We are advancing towards a nudist culture in the name of development, globalization and information revolution. Initially Russian channels forayed; they were banned for some time but later with aggressive percolation American and European media despoiled our family fool box where hitherto religious and didactic programs aired mainly. With the passing of time we also became habitual and halfheartedly tried to attain the pace of the era. Our own entertainment industry stepped into same shoes. We have to look here and there when such situations arise while watching television programs. Not only the movies which always stayed ahead in adopting and catering degraded and debauched material, but the other shows like serials and humour based also take liberty to expose us collectively.

Some years back I recall an occasion when a relative an aged one, was also watching some television show with us, perhaps it was a cricket match which is watched by everyone generally, otherwise elders avoid sitting and seeing collectively. Sticking to the television and watching whatever being shown is not more than a time killing exercise. In the meantime Liril soap

advertisement was aired during a break. We ignored it being some awkward situation and it was not so sensible to ogle it seriously but the old man saw with full interest the bikini girl dancing, jumping and diving in the swimming pool. We observed it obliquely. But he, the wise man uttered the words, 'it is not the summer time' (Ib kaunsi karsah hai). As though he was thinking and worrying about the health of the gracious modeling girl.

CHAPTER 10

50. Hopes of Hospitality

A name should depict the character, the attitude, the mental level of a person, but it doesn't apply every time and on each person. Though his name was Chatra, means a clever fellow, but he was a plain, simple and less level headed guy. He hardly attended a school, his adulthood passed grazing the livestocks and in other agrarian activities, nevertheless he was social and of gregarious nature. He was very much fond of feasting festivities, and generally represented his family in marriage banquets joyously, and even joined the baraat, the marriage party, with more fervor. In such a baraat at a village Masudpur, he had enjoyed and experienced the warm welcome and greetings in a great way. The hosts were attending them with folded hands and full appreciations. He observed the eatables arriving at the Chaupal, community centre, in a conventional manner and to his taste. Two persons carrying a big basket full of donas, pouches of sweets and confectionery, another two lifting a big brass vessel of hot tea with a braided cloth. A person was also carrying nearly hundred metal glasses intersinking each other in the shape of a bamboo stick. Thus Chatra was overwhelmed by the care and respect given by the hosts in every manner.

After a few days later he was on the way to the village of his relative carrying a bullock. Masudpur was on the

same route, just before the village he had to reach. When Masudpur came he remembered all the hospitalities received earlier at that place and walked to the same chaupal, tethered his bullock to the barred gate. He waited for some time at the chaupal, expecting the earlier treatment, but nobody turned up, irritatingly he left the place and made his way to the destination. On his return at home his fellow villagers enquired about the wellness of his visited region. He told dejectedly, "it is not like it had been, even Masudpur had changed." (pahlyan wali baat to Masudpur mein bhi nahin rah ri).

51. He was called Panda

It is believed about the Kumbh Mela that nectar drops fell from a pitcher, the kumbh, which is carried by the gods, in the rivers at four places, Hardwar, Allahabad, Nasik and Ujjain, The nectar was transpired from the sea churning. Bathing in these holy rivers is performed to cleanse the sins. It is a matter of belief for the Hindus. The pilgrims in Multitudes congregate at these places every third years consecutively. It is a passion for a Hindu to have a bath, the Snan on these auspicious occasions.

A chubby person in our village was called Panda, the Panda Pandit. I came to know in later years that there was an interesting interpretation about that name. As a holy dip in Ganga river at Hardwar is customary in this region to redeem the life's sins. A number of people from the village visit Hardwar every year to perform such ritual of 'Ganga Snan'. That guy, about whom I am talking, went to a Panditji to take specific advice about the holy dip. The Pandit ji advised him that the appropriate manner of

Ganga Snan was that he had to relinquish his old clothes with the flow of Ganga, while taking holy dip, chanting 'Har Har Gange, Har Har Gange'.

The gentleman comprehended all things and he carried a new dress of kurta dhoti in a fabric bag. On reaching Hardwar he placed the fabric bag on the bank of the river and stepped into the cold water enchanting the mantras simultaneously. He also surrendered the clothes one by one which he was wearing in the flow of water. Then he came out of the river and looked for the bag which was already stolen by the thieves unfortunately. Now the person was naked and penniless. A Panda showed mercy on his awkward predicament and gave him necessary clothes which fitted his plump body. He reached the village in Panda's outfit. From that day, everybody calls him a Panda.

52. Watching First Movie

I often sit and deliberate with the elderly people and listen to the things they are interested to share. They hold the treasure of experiences and also pleasing and practical talks of the past. They have passed through all the tasks and tantrums in which we have to go through, varied only by the time impact. Last year I passed a few moments with uncle Basau. After exchanging general courtesies I asked him about the films he had watched. I was surprised to know that he had seen several movies of his time. Then I wanted to know about the film he had seen for the first time. He tried to recollect the name but he couldn't, reason being it happened long ago and said much water had flown in Ganges and it is impossible to remember the particular name of a movie. But he elaborated the circumstances and incidents related to his maiden occasion of visiting a theatre.

He recalled that in those days he does the buffalo herding in the open land and often called in the village retreat where an ascetic lived. There was ample time to relax because the quadruped didn't create much trouble to be looked after. He developed cordial relations with the young ascetic. One day they planned to watch the night show of a movie in the theatre. So they reached the cinema hall and bought the tickets. He fluidly remembered that the movie was about two brothers who got separated in a fair and one became a robber with the passing of time. He also appreciated the beauty of heroine and praised her dance grinningly. He told about the strange incident which happened with them that night. When they came out of the theatre it was late enough, a policeman stared them for a few moments and then stopped them and enquired about their queer relationship. He then explained to the policeman with his sustained throaty voice, "I am Basau, a herder and often puff hubbly bubbly, the hookah with this ascetic living in the retreat, who desired to see movie and now we both are in your capture, that was the relationshiip." (bus yu mel thha).

53. Unplanned Constructions

A city has its limits to afford people within its territory, beyond which everything becomes chaotic. A great rush creates a number of problems, not only the general amenities become insufficient but an atmosphere of disrespect to common rules, the lawlessness, insecurity and other things raise their heads. The traffic bumps with each other, incidents of road rage often begin to take place. peace and serenity becomes distant dreams. There is a continuous exodus from the villages towards the townships, due to which all perspective planning is proving worthless. Nobody have estimated the number of vehicles India would have in the coming years, if planners had thought so then such jams wouldn't have taken place every day and throughout the year. There is a dire need of parallel planning of towns and villages. In India planned cities are many but there is no planned village. I think it will never be in near future. I don't know there is any plan in the offing. Even the 'lal dora' lands have no registry facility and the occupiers hold the rights of the properties.

General constructions are raised haphazardly. Encroachments of common lands are done widely. At a time several ponds were there around the villages, these all are occupied by the adjoining families or who hold some clout. The streets which should be of justifiable width are now tight enough to pass and due to heavy encroachments no street is straight. It is very cumbersome to cross a village. People often talk complainingly and meetings on such issues prove inconclusive. I myself was a witness in a village meeting which was called to discuss the problem of encroachment and difficulties faced by all. Different pleas and points were placed and so many suggestions evolved. The stumbling block was the involvement of all, be it issues of foundations or projections. A person called Dutta was silent throughout the proceedings. Everybody looked towards Dutta for his valuable suggestion. Dutta said in the end, "The whole village should be demolished once by a road roller, and then it should be reconstructed with a wider planning."

54. The Tractor Craze

His royal arch (nora) had never been empty throughout the year. A tractor always could be seen standing majestically there. I am talking of uncle Basau who was crazy after tractors and inclined to buy the secondhand machinery. He readily bought any assortment, it might be practical or not but prices should be dirt cheap and manageable. His conversations were afloat with tractors, convincing practicalities, different brand names, its spares and specifications. Many mechanics were his close friends, day in or day out they were to be called to keep going his second hand tractors, people often saw the opened engines and other parts of the structure, and they became accustomed to listen the penetrating start trial sounds in the serene atmosphere of the village.

He was also wont to sell and buy another tractor regularly, sometimes unique one, for which he faced difficulties on unavailability of spares and expertise. Fellow villagers frequently advised him to retract the hold view of purchasing the used one, for it is hard to maintain the older machinery and also it is ungainly. Then he took a bold decision and bought a brand new tractor, it was Sartaj; a brand name, also a distinctive one in the village and it was some sort of dwarfing model. Unreasonable low spiritedness was visible enough on uncle's face after a few days. Then one day people noticed him without tractor and they talked him in general way about the empty royal arch (nora). He disclosed that he had sold the tractor, for it was not suitable to his stature. Another shortcoming was that it didn't run fast, and its slow speed was irritating enough which he realized later. He told, "Nobody asked him while climbing up or climbing down." (na koi chadte hue puchhe thha na uterte hue).

CHAPTER 11

55. Tree the Prosperity

More trees in the farm are certainly the sign of prosperity. You may observe that the farmer who plants trees every year seems strong financially, mentally and also socially. For he is a person worth talking in the village. His planning is discussed throughout the community. What to talk about a person who doesn't grow even a single tree, He even shelters at noon under a neighbour's tree. By destroying the flora we are missing the colourful birds because they have lost their natural habitat. We generally argue the use of more chemicals for the extinction of beautiful creatures. Why don't we accept that we are the reasons behind the destruction of birds' home? We have cut the natural cycle, the birds who ate the harmful bugs are no more, pests are thriving due to dearth of predators. Result is the crop infection and the farmers have to resort to the use of pesticides, the chemicals, which directly or indirectly affect our lives, more human diseases are originating.

Main problem is if a tree is cut nobody plants another, keep the land naked. A farmer's argument against the shadowy tree is that it is detrimental to the crop growth, but there is vast region in India where both plants and crops are flourishing in tandem. They haven't kept the cereals and fruits against each other, both are placed parallel as cash crops. I know a person who has toured globally. He often talks about Europe and its prosperity, I like when he talks about Belgium a smaller and beautiful country, he dwells upon its attractions which strikes me. He said Belgium is a country which is full of fruit trees. He wandered widely and saw that there are fruit trees on the main roads, express highways, along with railway tracks, on the banks of the rivers and streams, even along with smaller water channels. There is the splendid beauty of fruits dangling on the shrubs even in the human settlements. One may just imagine about the gorgeousness of the nation and also about the health of the people.

56. The Sting of a Mosquito

A mosquito's sting is not a sting in reality. It is an injection and it takes the blood from our body by suction. Its mechanism is not a defensive mechanism like of a wasp which attacks anticipating danger to life. He is feeding himself upon us. Initially he applies anesthesia for not to be caught taking blood. Anesthesia works for a short period and the mosquito flies away after sipping, and then starts the irritating pain in our body. Of course there are sluggish mosquitoes who continue suction without caring for time and effect of anesthesia. They are killed by our slapping attack. The moral is that the passive always die first just like a greedy bribe taker.

These things are happening around us and with us. A sting of corruption and extortion is being injected with or without anesthesia. Every types of reforms are instantly thwarted by the fraudulent fiddlers. There is a plethora of rules and acts to tackle it, but all efforts are made redundant and defunct by the debased and perverted people. The evaders of law don't abjure from their ill doings and continue to trim the entrails of the system. The anesthesia is being smeared to the common man, resulting in no serious complaints from the public and bribery goes on thriving incessantly without interruption. The crooked officials evolve new tricks to extract the payola.

It is said that the grafting starts from top to bottom, they deploy their orderlies to garner the gravy from the flatland. These smaller rivulets turned into larger flows and streams, bounties go on increasing and amassing. It is also evident that a crusader against corruption is achieving the most. The corruption issue is so much effective that it has remained pivotal in the government coup every time, The shrewd person always has reached at the helm of affairs by making a common man daydreaming, swindling them in daylight but fundamental changes are nowhere in sight. The commoners have to bear the pain when the effects of anesthesia diminish.

57. The Timely Reforms

There is a sea change in society, security, study and even in schooling. Literacy rate was minimal, well to do families too didn't show much interest in sending their children to schools. Corporal punishment was prevalent in those days, many of the children had a fright about the teacher's cane, and teachers also postulated the theory that learning was not possible without thrashing; it was one of the reasons of renouncing learning for several youngsters. As the country was cash-strapped, so were the people. The schemes which are floated today were not in the older days, although such schemes were required at that time. There was no term like free education and more or less monthly fee had to be paid from the first standard, school uniform had to be bought and there was no provision of nutritional meal and we had to sprint in the recess time to have our lunch. It can be construed that our schooling was a paid learning as the parents of this age boasts about the private schooling of their children.

Another thing was that, there was screening at every standard, annual examination system was functional and results were announced on a fixed date and students failed in substantial numbers. State Board conducted the middle examinations and that was arduous enough for the majority of students, many used to drop their study at this level due to repeatedly failing. I remember a fellow who failed five times continuously. The document received by a failure student was called a blacklist; it was of the size of a ration card that was also called a permit in villages. I saw other juveniles chiding him by christening him a permit holder. Work training started from the very beginning, from the childhood, we regularly helped our parents in their day to day tasks, from farming to the livestock rearing and that proved to be advantageous for the health. The man who worked physically was seen as a highly esteemed person and idleness was watched with derision, If someone tried to be a work shirker he was pronounced as a 'doom' a person known for his slothfulness, who sustains himself on begging or praising others.

58. Everybody should Grow Plants

Just imagine there is no government land in a city in India. Think there is no government educational institution, no government office building, of course they may be in private hired constructions. There is no colony developed by public sector. This will certainly affect the issues of communism, socialism and equal opportunity in the first place. But what I see the first impact would be on ecosystem. Whatever plantation and trees are there, these are on government land. If there is any open space, parks and greenery, it is mainly on public land. Health of public would be in jeopardy directly.

One of the reasons of birds' gradual extinction is apathy of human beings towards the plantations of fruit trees. Early morning while walking, melodious voices may be heard. The showy lush green and non-deciduous plants like Alestonia, Balamkhira etc. do not attract birds due to their poisonous nature. On the other hand Jamun, Chikoo and even peepal shelter these lovely creatures.

While coming out or entering in the house I regularly see towards the branches of Jamun tree which is growing in my front tiny garden. In spite of vagaries of weather and perpetual attacks by monkeys the Jamuns go on ripening. It is matter of fillip that these grow in bunches like grapes. It is a sense of pleasance that is felt every time to observe the fruits developing, maturing and ripening. I also take it as a supplement on my part to the larger pleasing environment.

The twi-twi melodious voice in the chikoo tree at my backyard was coming for few days. I tried to see the bird between the dense green leaves in futile. Four days ago I spotted a lovely bulbul, sitting calmly, no chirping. Through these days she was busy in her work. She was weaving a nest. It is now big enough to be seen between fruits and foliage. We hope more such voices would be heard after a few days. These are really pleasing moments.

59. The Fundamental Flaws

I don't think there is any country in the World where there are so much political discussions except India. There are whole timers who throughout the year just talk politics. They chase the MPs and MLAs and their activities in such a way that there remains no chance for a representative to take any innovative step even if he had thought so. There is a fundamental dearth of positivity and guarded polemics. There is a majority of population which has nothing to do with politics, they are busy in their drudgery of day to day work and largely are hand to mouth, but these simple fellows are also dragged into it and simultaneously exploited by the smart leaders who are opportunistic. There are layers of elections from the lower level to the upper level and some sort of voting always remains in pipeline and also a gist of material for time consuming conversations is every time at hand. I don't think there is least productivity factor in such exercises. Of course elections are integral phenomena in a democratic set up but it is becoming indulging.

The persons who are active in politics are largely lacking in expertise and don't have any concrete policy and planning for the upliftment of the poor population. The whole exercise has become farce. The living standard of a common man hardly improves in five years tenure but a member of parliament or a legislator attains an aristocratic position within these five years. Certainly there are fundamental flaws in the system which should be addressed. Maximum politicians in India are whole time politicians. Their calling is politics. You can imagine the limit of political talks that just after electing one government, the next day we start talking who will win after five years. Idleness is unlimited.

CHAPTER 12

60. Ascetics in the Village

There lived two ascetic persons in our village, One inhabited alone at a small retreat adjoining the village, I had never seen anyone as his disciple. Some youngsters often visited him at his retreat just to puff hubble-bubble in the afternoon or for some voluntary service. We called him 'kutti wala baba', the ascetic at retreat. I observed him as a fully satisfied person, a saintly figure, beyond all worldly things, quite reticent in nature, beyond sorrow and happiness. He seldom went to the village for alms, hardly once in a month, people willingly offered foodstuffs more than his requirements. I later realized he was doing a great job for the community, he blew shankh, the conch just at the setting of sun and in the tranquil atmosphere of the village, its sound was heard throughout the settlement. Listening to this curious sound I saw people acknowledging that it was time to recall the god and uttered the name 'Ramji' heartedly. Women folks lightened the earthen lamps at the same time.

Another baba, a man of full anatomy allotment lived at the community building, the chaupal. He attired himself in loose fitting saffron clothes. I noticed him not as a devout but seemingly religious, he often visited his family at a distantly located village. He was a social fellow and mingled even with children who gathered at the chaupal to play. This baba traversed the whole village, went every house daily for alms (jyani) He generally asked for the wheat flour, but on Sundays he accepted the crude butter only, we often watched him in chaupal, purifying it by heating, tried to shove us away. In later years he began to accept other cereals also. Women often asked him for the choice of the grains to be given. Baba used to reply, "I haven't any silo (kuthhla) for different grains, you can bestow anything, and it all would be sold to the shopkeeper."

61. The Roles of a Styler

Some customs are not only unique but watchable. Deep penetrated caste system again and again erupts and shows its face at many occasions. The role of a styler in a marriage ceremony makes us remember that such caste patterns, gradations and supremacy will continue for a long time. An upper caste fellow might bring the stacks of fodder from his field for his domesticated animals, placing on his head throughout the year, but he certainly engages a styler to carry a trunk containing valuable articles on the occasions of weddings. A styler or hajam in a village does not do the work of hairdressing and shaving only but he is a person who performs multiple duties like messengering, portering and inviting people for someone's function. Be it the occasion of celebrations or mourning a styler's role is significant enough. I remember in my village, a styler, besides being a marginal tiller used to perform all the assignments of a general styler.

During the season of marriages his activities became too hectic. He sent the turmeric immersed wedding missive written by a purohit to bride's or bridegroom's house as the case might be. He wandered house to house to invite people for special feast. He changed his working vigorously, He prepared the baraatis by shaving and hairdressing in large numbers, his duty changed into a porter when the baraat reached at bride's house, lifted the trunk containing valuables like jewelry, walked ahead of the procession. But he broadly visited the houses to beautify the faces, even he reached the ranches to shave off the farmers in lieu of a stack of fodder. His scissors and razors were of substandard quality, people often saw him whetting his razors at the main bridge of the canal. Once he started to shave a farmer with a blunt razor, making him grumble, 'why don't you wet my chin?' The styler retorted, "Don't worry, I will elicit the water from your eyes." (pani to ankhyan mein tai kad layunga).

62. The Mule Carter

It is not an exaggeration to call a potter a group of companies because a potter in a village not only does the work of pottery but he delivers numerous services to the society. Firstly he manufactures the earthenwares for the whole village, initiating by giving shape to raw porous soil and then firming up in fire of low and continuous heat. Secondly he is a transporter from the ancient times using a mule cart and his honesty is renowned in this arena, whatever you hand over to the mule carter, it will certainly reach to the right place in full and secure. Thirdly a potter is also a manufacturer of bricks in the same way as he prepares the earthenwares. He has extended the use of his mule cart in buying the commodities from one area selling at other places. In this way he is stepping up as a businessman gradually. But his mule cart has always been in the central place because in all his various professions portering is required.

While doing graduation I was often intercepted by the mule carts which used to run between the town and my village. Before the regular bus service to my village I had to walk five kilometres to catch a bus from a neighbouring village. It was far good to utilize such conveyances to save time. I always avoided sitting and waiting for a motorbus for a long time and started to walk. Many a time I chanced to get a private vehicle otherwise it would be a good stroll in a company or solitarily. Though soon bus began plying but I maintained my older routine for some time due to lesser rounds of the bus. That day I took a lift from a mule carter Hari, a potter of my village and soon got into conversation with him saying, "It is good a bus has started plying to our village. He showed no excitement to my statement but he said worryingly, "Now my animal wouldn't get peace on this road!" (ib pashu ne aaram koni).

63. Registered Medical Practitioner

The doctor in our village wandered throughout the village, on anybody's call from to corner of the habitation. In those days malaria attacked people largely, in and around rainy season. There were rarest of families in the village where there was no malaria patient. On the simple message, the local doctor, probably a registered medical practitioner whom we called doctor uncle visited our house. He checked the patient by the wrist vein, sensed its throbbing, as we comprehended, but it was more about feeling the temperature and diagnosing. Immediately he used to declare it as malaria, gave some pills to lower the body temperature, in order to give injection. People took it a definite remedy to recover, simple pills were less relied. There were no dangers of infectious diseases that time and using the single syringe and needle on multiple persons was common, he just demanded a glass of fresh water to clean the syringe and needle. He himself emboldened the patient who had a needle fright.

I never noticed him asking money for treatment, he treated people on credit, received his fee at the harvesting season. He was a tailor simultaneously, he visited the patients in the morning or at evening, and he sewed clothes in between. He served whole village community for a long time, one or two such practitioners also tried their luck but couldn't sustain longer against him and his pleasing and social demeanor. Another practitioner also came in our village who was physically lean and lanky, people soon began to take him lightly and indifferently. Once a guy accosted him about availability of the energy capsules (takat ki dawa). The doctor replied that there were plenty of such capsules and how much he required. At this the man quipped, "Then why don't you take yourself?" Sometimes varoom varoom of a motorcycle was heard, people knew that he was a doctor called from the town, revealing somebody's serious condition, otherwise local doctor uncle was competent enough to handle the general diseases.

CHAPTER 13

64. The Quilt and the Saang

In a village a Saang (dance drama) was being performed in the season of severe cold. Saang had been a very popular medium of entertainment in rural folks. In it, a story is told in an entertaining way with impressive dialogues, songs and dances by the troupers on the four corners of a pedestal. A Nakli (buffoon) is also an integral part of Saang who amuses the viewers with his buffoonery. People walked several miles at night to watch a Saang. It was crushing season of sugarcane also. A farmer was going to the indigenous crusher to crush his sugarcanes with his two yolked bullocks and a folded quilt on his head in order to save him from harsh chill. They reached to the crusher by approximation of their turn called Kundi. In the midway he was tempted to have some entertainment for a short time in the Saang. Soon he absorbed himself fully in the enchanting songs, the enticing plot and hilarious frivolity of the clown. In the serenity of night a melodious atmosphere was created by the performers by their various musical instruments.

In the meantime there was a commercial break in which people endowed donations in the form cash and kinds, sometimes competitions evolved between different givers of such largesse. In that competition of bestowing of gifts, that farmer also staked his quilt and gifted it to the thespians in the flare up atmosphere.

Then he reached at the crusher where he had to wait a while for his turn (Kundi). Without quilt he was feeling intense chilling and realized his blunder. He drew in the pile of bagasse to protect himself from the chilling cold. The poker came to collect the fuel for furnace and as he inclined to take the armful of bagasse, he was frightened to notice the hidden man and cried, "Who is there?" The poor guy replied, "Brother, I am a victim of charity." (bhai, mein hun danan ka maryo)

65. Untouchability

Untouchability prevailed in our society for a long time. We all have witnessed such scenes and situations. The farmers hired people from lower classes for ploughing and livestock herding. But they were called 'Siri' (partners) and not servants in order to give them due respect. They were partners in real sense, because they had to do the same work what the farmers did. They accomplished all the farming works collectively. In spite of all, there used to be separate utensils for them for having a meal and there were not much objections on this issue from either side. Literacy made substantial difference in this direction. A literate does not care about untouchability more. Knowledge and cognition eroded this traditional evil from the society.

I recall a teacher from my village, who happened to be a farmer simultaneously, hired a person as a herder for his buffaloes. The herder belonged to a lower caste eventually. But the teacher farmer was open-minded, and he should be, being a teacher who enlightens the public. In the afternoon when the herder came driving the buffaloes, he faced the teacher sitting on a cot. who had just returned from his work, the imparting of education. Here the hilarious situation arises. The herder with the idea of untouchability in his mind, demanded water to quench his thirst from the teacher. The teacher with a smile on his face retorted, "Gentleman, I am not your attendant, but you are mine, so you take the water from the pitcher and also fetch a glass for me."

66. Dignitary as a Balloon Seller

In a neighbouring village a fair was being held every year on the festival of Rakshabandan. We planned it early to enjoy it most, the list of toys to be bought, and the eatables to be savoured. The budget had been circumscribed and the annual hike was also nominal, but our aspirations multiplied each year, the things which could not be purchased previous year, we intended to have them at the coming occasion. Basically the fair was organized to commemorate some anniversary of a saint and people reached there to worship and have blessings, but I couldn't see the altar in the crowd and also hardly desired so. We visited the fair for fun, the tamasha, acrobatics, the indigenous casters, the men continually jumping and pushing trolleys down, the monkey shows, the snake charmers and other pageants interesting enough.

The akharas, wrestling rings attracted more spectators. From the bantamweight to the heavyweight, numerous grapplers were seen challenging, circling in the ring simultaneously tapping their thighs, a connotation for assertion and challenge. Someone from the gathering might jump and accept the fight and the bout started, the winners received the cash rewards from the assemblage. In the evening after returning from the fair discussions ensued. One of them said he saw a dignitary of the village selling balloons in the fair. Others refuted it and said it was impossible, why should he sell balloons. He was right, actually what happened, the dignitary wanted to purchase balloons for his six grandsons. The balloon seller who was holding a bamboo stick fixed with balloons, demanded one and half rupees for six balloons from the old man, the dignitary. He gave a fifty rupee note to the balloon hawker. The balloon seller decamped with the fifty rupee note saying he was arranging the change. While going he handled the balloon fixed bamboo stick to the dignitary who waited for the imposter for a long time. People took him as an actual seller.

67. Saang, the Dance Drama

I haven't seen much Saangs, the dance dramas but whichever have seen it was a nice entertaining experience on the whole. Largely these Saangs were invited to perform at a village in order to collect some amount besides entertainment motive. The target might be to construct a community school or to achieve some collective purpose in which money is needed. Generally Saangs were enacted at night when the rural folks were at ease after completing their farming tasks in daytime. Usually this form of art was known by the head of the troupe called Saangi, a man of authority on the stage and all the Saangis had the common stories and they performed it with mutatis mutandis, the alterations were made mainly in the lyrics, the raganis. Their system of performing was superb, a pedestal of considerable height was prepared in a square shape, nearly dozen people cuddled together on it. The audiences in large numbers from several villages used to sit all around it.

There were various sorts of artists like the drummers, and the drums were also of different sizes, the trumpeters, long fork type of instruments, the harmoniums, the indigenously prepared beating drum, an earthen pot, its opening fitted with flexible tube etc. All thespians were male members, including four dancers, attired as women folks and looked charming, who danced on the four corners of the pedestal in tandem. I couldn't understand why the younger dancer was called the sweet candy (mithhi goli) every time. The main artist advanced the tale with the help of songs and narratives. I saw people spellbound on raganis and dance in tandem at four corners. But I always preferred the narratives which pushed the story ahead. A clown, the nakli was also an eminent part of the saang who entertained the spectators in between, with his peculiar jokes and caricatures. Saangs were started late, enough to make you sleepy. In addition the most tiring and boring was the recitation 'You and your name are supreme' (tuhi tuhi tera naam sahi), invoking the goddess of music for a long time.

68. Skinflints

A person buys a Popsicle from a vendor and relishes its taste and temperature for a long time until a wooden stick remains in his hand. Yet he doesn't throw the spike, places it in his pocket and restores it in his home, keeping in view its advantages in coming times. He claims that the left over wooden stick will be useful in putting a string in a pyjama. We can think about his visionary thinking. Another person who is walking on a road, finds a dropped pedal of a bicycle. He at once picks it up to take him to his house. His son questions him about its feasibility and he answers that one day they will fix a bicycle in it. We can just imagine about his future thinking and optimism. Society calls them skinflints, scrooges and tightwads. But one thing is clear that they entertain the society in a great deal by their weird doings.

A miser type of person is very calculative. He always has a fear of losing money. That doesn't mean he is unsocial or unfriendly. But he is smart enough to deal with social affairs. His tendency is to cope with the world with lesser money. He might be very choosy in his expenditure. Once during a visit of Chandigarh such guy was in my company, of course a close friend. At lunchtime; when we entered a hotel which was of more than medium standard. My friend feared about the ensuing hefty bill and immediately told me that he had no money. I said, "Why are you worrying." The waiter came to take orders for our meal. Then I ordered like this, "Bring for me a shahi paneer and a plain paneer for my poor friend." (mere liye ek shahi paneer aur iske liye ek nang paneer). Because the poor guy has no money.

69. Biting by a Snake

It is said about snakes that all are not poisonous and there are a few species which are more harmful and even may pose danger to life. In villages people know more about these creatures and talk about them for hours. At several times it becomes main issue of discussions. They know by the colour of a snake about its ferociousness. It is also common view that a snake which feeds on earth or a water snake or even double headed are not so much perilous, but the snakes of dry lands that live in earthen mounds are more insidious and might cause grievous results. Snakes of dark colours like cobra and king cobra are famous for their their severe and venomous attacks. Anti-venom serums are prepared by the venom itself. There are conventional methods of healing of snake bites.

Once a person was bitten by a snake at night while he was watering his crops and couldn't see the snake which bit him. Two cuts mark is the sure symptom of the venomous attack. He tried its remedy in nearby villages and at last he was recommended to consult a snakebite healer who used to cure the patient by enchanting special mantra. So he reached to such a healer. The healer inspected the cuts and said, "there are different fees for different types of snakebites. If you are bitten by earthen feeder I will enchant a mantra which will cost you rupees ten and if you are attacked by a double headed then you have to pay rupees twenty. I have another two mantras of rupees fifty and rupees hundred each which are applied on healing snakebites by cobra and king cobra respectively."

The healer said to the stung patient that he had to decide which mantra he wanted to be recited accordingly. The patient, a penny pincher thought the healer was trying to swindle him by different rates of mantras. He even doubted that the healer had multiple mantras. So the patient told him casually that he had been stung by an earthen feeder and gave him a ten rupee note. When the healer started to enchant mantra the patient felt apprehensive of his cure, because he was doubtful about the species of the biting snake. He interrupted him by saying, "please tag one or two mantras of king cobra in between." (ek aadh bich bich mein kala ka bhi aane de).

CHAPTER 14

70. The Dummy Cat

Have you ever been vexed by the mice menace? I have. From where does the mouse enter my car? No clue is striking me and not to my mechanic. Although I left my vehicle with him for the whole day to find out the open hole, he detailed me about all the muddles, which he had thoroughly inspected and found them fixed. He advised me not to park the vehicle around the food grains but it was already not the situation. There is open land in front of my house where wild plants thrive; burrows in the groves are discernible. Someone guided me to keep the bonnet open in order to normalize the temperature of the car, the mice will not find it warming, will seek another house to be comfy. This suggestion also proved a non-starter. Again I found the mouse traces in the morning within the vehicle like nibbling of the mats and even faecal balls of the gnawer.

Then I purchased a mice trap, set bait in the crooked wire at night. In the morning I met a chubbier creature with whiskers. I opened the cage to free him cautiously at a comfortable distance from my house lest it might return. Next day again, there was one more mouse in the trap, but faecal balls were again spotted on the front seat. Probably there was another one who wandered in the car leaving one in the trap. There was an alternative for it, I bought such a mice trap, which could capture several mice at night. I got respite for a few days but the mice menace arose again. I sought remedies from everyone. Mothballs were also suggested by a person, for these would prove repellent to the rodents, I placed the mothballs here and there, even inside the car, these worked for a long time, but soon they became habitual to its effect.

Another proposal came of the peppermint oil, for its odour is unbearable to rats. I used a swab, soaked in the peppermint oil every night, putting it at the dashboard. It remained effective only for a few days, now the rats began gnawing the interior of the car including wires. Last week a formidable idea struck in my mind. I bought a dummy cat from the market and placed it, not in an ambush position, but under the car facing the main entrance of the house, from where the rodents enter stealthily. Of course there is dark but a cat can see in the darkness, so does the mouse. Yes, it is really working.

71. Music my Fascination

Music charms me more than anything else, provided it should be distinct. I always try to venture into different types of euphony. Golden ages of Hindi songs have been camouflaged by the Punjabi folks due to their sudden surge and popular approach to the common man. Through this form of art rich Punjabi literature have received attention and people attracted to it, there was also a vacuum of definitive Hindi songs and that situation was fully utilized by the inherent artistic Punjabis. I often listen melodies of Harjit Harman who sings Pargat Singh's songs. These songs carry substantive meaning along with soothing music, they relate not only the great history of undivided Punjab but realistic situations also. Gurdas Mann, the legendary figure floated a distinctive genre in music by exploring the less feminine path. Babbu Mann the choosiest singer, has been compared to Michael Jackson in Punjab due to his uncompromising nature in music. I like his exalted imagery in his lyrics. In one song he compares the damsel's eyes with Osama Bin Laden (ankhian laden bargi, jeda jatke je dunia hilade).

Hayanvi music also fascinates me and keeps a peculiar collection of ragnis and folk songs. I am also inclined to classical instrumental music, listen Tabla and flute. I often engrossed in the Tabla maestro Zakir Hussein's playing 'thhak dina din' and flutist Hari Parsad Chaurasia make me captive by his soothing symphony. I acquired the renowned duo in a single concert and frequently listen a blend of Tabla and flute, particularly while driving. In one of the journeys three ladies were also travelling with me on the back seat, I continued listening the classical duo for a long time with anticipation that everyone was enjoying the music. I halted at a place and asked the ladies for refreshments. One of them thanked me and also requested to stop the cacophony for it was hollowing her temple. (meri to khopri khhali kar di).

72. The Monotonous Game

We aspire variations, we seek new things, we search newer places, we intend to add relations with different people, and we desire to relish fresh foods and eatables. But all such things don't apply on study, I always felt it boring and tiring to read a book and even a topic again and again, avoided going near the material which I studied once, preferred passing my time under the shady trees adjoining canteen where there was always an entertaining assemblage of likeminded students. Though it has been made fundamental for higher scoring in examinations. It is said that one should go through an article repeatedly to perceive it and reproduce it at the examination time, and I have observed the readers studying continually and incessantly. My roommate always did that untiringly and used to advise me to do so for better achievements, although whenever I tried to read something second time I felt blank and collapsed. His repeating inclinations provided me a clean and tidy room. He washed not only his clothes but many a time mine also. A guest left his dress inadvertently; my roommate placed it after good washing and ironing.

Once he developed some toothache problem. So he visited a dentist who happened to be a lady doctor. On his return I asked him what the doctor concluded about his toothache. He told that some filling was required and the dentist had done that. But he visited the doctor two to three times more. I asked him about his recurring visits. He told me that he had made filling of two more teeth. l questioned the propriety and extravagances. He explained, "he needed filling more or less and so long as charges are concerned he has to bear half of the charges and half the payment is recovered when the doctor inclines and cascades her hair down." What an explanation !

73. Traveling by a Bus

Travelling by bus is a unique experience in itself. You will gain enough even from a journey of one hour. Sometimes strangers will apprise you so many things, you need not to indulge directly, but there are such people who always talk in high pitched voice and you can overhear them. You will strike an array of people in the compact space of a bus. Someone may start elaborating about various religious things, perhaps you wouldn't have bothered to know earlier, but they would certainly provide you the basics of customs and conventions. At another time, someone may impinge on with quackery knowledge and might start to elaborate the herbal remedies of some sort of unwellness. These types of persons are seen having more attentive listeners, being intercepted with some personal queries intermittently. Grueling and grumblings against the system are also ever existing phenomena. Political debaters often, suddenly come to the fore fighting for partisan interests, at certain occasions leading to heated exchanges. The hawkers' activities are entertaining enough while selling practical objects in a highly flaunting and facetious style.

If you are a daily commuter, your relationships grow more than familiarity, with the fellow passengers. Even the bus staffers become enough intimating. When we, students from my village, were studying in college, daily bus journey remained an exciting exercise for us. Bus service was limited and it was often overcrowded. We had to run to catch and enter into it, took it as a challenging task. The distance which should have been covered in twenty minutes, it consumed double duration of time. The driver an old man drove it too slow, entertaining public, halting at numerous places, even clambered down several times to clear the road which often thronged by the quadrupedal animals. One day we were dismayed to listen that the driver had a double vision problem, and asked him why the gentleman had not applied for the premature retirement. He told us that he had forwarded such request. He had shared his plight with the authority that it was becoming difficult to drive because he was seeing two roads ahead. The officer declined his appeal amusingly, saying, "Drive on the better one." (badiya wali sadak pe chalale).

CHAPTER 15

74. Migrants

Let's add something more in Christ's teachings 'blessed are those whose kith and kins live abroad'. The person who plans to go abroad is certainly a visionary, who has some dreams to realize, who seeks opportunities sacrificing the love of the family at home. At a distant land a man has to relinquish the pride which he nurture at his own place, humbleness prevails upon him and that opens the gates of progress. Generally people have made progress more; who are in foreign lands. Some of them are luminous enough and have touched the peak positions of leading global companies. The states which send more people outside are flourishing like Kerala where Dinar is flowing down from the Arab countries and lifestyle of the Keralites has improved and elevated. But most perceptible progress can be noticed in Punjab, where nearly from every village the Punjabis have migrated to the developed countries, and uplifted the overall economy of the state.

Punjab matches to many European nations in many measures. Euros and Dollars are being syphoned and received by the common households. The laborious Punjabis earned more and have strengthened the family positions back at their ancestral villages. A person who was sending money handsomely every month to his wife returned from abroad after a long time. When he rose in the morning what he watched, a number of servants had been engaged by his wife, and there came the sweeper, the mopper, the cook and the washer man. He was surprised to see a number of helping hands and said to his wife, "What an irony! There I mop and here you have hired a mopper." Once I asked my friend whose cousin was also in USA," Is he sending enough money at home?" My friend told, "He often writes letters to us, we read it thoroughly, from the beginning to the end, and there is never mention of dollars or rupees, his letters are largely about weather report."

75. The Life Long Tussle

Both had a great respect for each other. Their mutual caring and affection was often talked in the village. I am talking of two brothers, named Banwari and Girdhari, both were hard working as well as adjusting. Their cooperation and team work contributed to the flourishing crops on the farm and that ensued the prosperity of the family. But things don't go coherent and smooth forever, suspicions and misconceptions beget discordance. Both started quarreling on petty issues which were earlier neglected and unnoticed. Both began brandishing lathis on minor bickerings. Trespassing by one's cattle, irrigation matters, encroachments, projections often led to violent fights between the two. Things went on aggravating with the passing of time, but they never tried to conciliate. These became habituated scenes for the villagers, often they enjoyed the regular clashes climbing on the rooftops.

The bloodshed continued undeterred between the two brothers. They crossed the age of eighty without abjuring animosity. And the time reached when the elder brother

Banwari fell ill and his condition went on deteriorating, he came on the death bed. Emotions erupted and he remembered his incessant tumultuous relations with his younger brother. He wanted to see him in his last moments. So Girdhari was called on his earnest will. He beseeched him that their life long tussle should not be extended to our offsprings after his demise, He said, "promise me, you would not afflict my sons after me." Girdhari assured him immediately, "Brother, die in peace, nothing will happen like this in future." On his reply, Banwari muttered in the end, I should not be remembered as a coward for I kept you cornered all life." (kamjor na layiye, tu sada kunn mein la ke rakhya).

76. The Dunaliman

Generally railway journey is dull and drab due to more strangeness and multitudinous of passengers and it cannot be approximated that to which region the commuter belongs. But many a time the environment changes in the compartment if there is anyone of garrulous temperament and such person breaks the ice, otherwise we just listen the shouts of the hawkers and the tea sellers intermittently. I am talking of those days when coal engines ran and you collected substantial amount of soot in your pockets while travelling. Once an interesting event occurred which I myself witnessed. There were many students in that compartment and also a gentleman with curled and heavy mustaches giving an impression of an authoritative personality. The guy was wearing rustic dress, a white tunic and lungi and a 'dunali' a double barrel gun was also slinging on his shoulder.

Everyone who passed through the gallery certainly had a look on the gun bearing man.

Soon some students began chattering with the brave man and he also framed interesting stories of courage and bravery. He proceeded forth by telling the specifications of the weapon and how it had been useful for him and then embarked on tales of shoving away the occupiers of plots and of freeing many lands. Soon the railway station reached where we as well as the dunaliman had to leave the train. What I saw there was a raid of traveling ticket examiners, the students in large numbers were caught without tickets, the officials fined them heavily and defiers were pushed into a van to be sent to jail. What was more spectacular, the gunner passenger had also not bought the ticket. Initially he tried some pretexts and bulling but the adventurous TTE caught him with the collar. That was a striking scene for everyone on the platform, a dunaliman was caught without ticket and the railway officers were pushing him inside the van with his gun slinging on his shoulder.

77. Stressed Relations

You meet hundreds of people in a day, outside your home, in society and it is not certain that all entertain you warmly, someone might exhibit a lukewarm attitude or even a rude posture, but you behave accordingly, making adjustments pertaining to your moods, your compulsions, your obligations, and pressure upon you, timings and your endurance. You accommodate and adapt in accordance with the situations. It is not only difficult but unfeasible to go on in existence without being conciliatory and mentally balanced. When traits like tolerance and insusceptibility erode from human disposition, disintegration of society and even family structure takes place. When inculcated goodness and graces are dismissed from mind, misfortune and jeopardy raise their heads. At the least the institutions of the house and the family should be sustained and nurtured, when you can cope with a tumultuous atmosphere, where multifarious afflictions prevail. You might bump in with an imposter; you might have to deal with a hypocrite, a trickster, even with a criminal. When you are compatible to exist in such adversities, it is effortless to be harmonious at home, the initial pillar of society.

I have intimate relations with him and have visited his house several times even after studies. So to say I am still a persona grata even for his parents. He had sent an invitation of his wedding but unfortunately I couldn't attend the ceremony, due to my other unavoidable engagements. I approached him at his home after six months and wanted to see his better half, but she was conspicuous by her absence and I thought she might have gone to her parents' home. He talked on several matters but I turned the topic on his marriage, which he was trying to avoid. He brought out the marriage album to show me but not in a cheerful mood, continued to turn over the pages with minor details. I was also seeing the photographs, with intermittent queries. I asked about an authoritative young man and his relations with him. He answered with some irritation, "This is my sala, yes sala (brother in law)" (ye mera sala hai sala). I comprehended the situation on his reiteration of the word 'sala'. Their marital relationship was already stressed.

CHAPTER 16

78. Traffic Sense

Traffic rule is one thing and traffic sense is another, but unfortunately rules, which are never enforced, are kept ahead. General public hardly know and are indifferent to learn the tedious rules. Largely people seek ways for avoidance of the regulations. Timed reviews of the rules are also essential, concerning the need of the hour and space on the roads. If our thrust is on disseminating the traffic sense, it ought to be favourable to perception, friendly, more practical and beneficial to everybody. Although traffic rules are limited and traffic sense is spread out, but it is adaptable. Driving etiquettes and conduct on road ordinarily are learnt mainly by experience, by going through it. Often a stranger will pass you giving tips by lovable methods and sometimes with piercing looks that will surely imprint on your mind, for you are receptive at that moment.

I recollect an incident from the earlier time. A few years back I was riding a motorbike on more than normal speed, more than which it should not be on a busy road. It is not imperative you are attentive enough while driving, so many things may find space in your mind. Suddenly I saw an old man was crossing a road and I apprehended that strike is imminent, for there was not enough time to control the bike, nevertheless I tried my best and there was a narrow escape with some skidding on the sidewalk, I felt frightening sensations momentarily. The cyclist gentleman came to me after balancing his bicycle on its stand, touched my right handlebar and uttered just these words "Young man, more you screw this, more it will run." (jitna isse gumaoge, utna hi tez dorega). I was just speechless.

79. A Shoe Shop

A shoe shop is unique in its furnishings and oneness of things, all shoe boxes are neatly arranged. Some benches are placed along one wall of the shop alongwith other things. In the midst of it, foot length assessors and wooden splinters to help you putting on the shoes for trials are scrambled. Most helpers in the store sit on mat covered floor, keep on trying the shoes, fitting with the help of wooden splinters simultaneously squalling the names of different brands and measurements towards the square hole in the centre of the ceiling. These salespersons recount continuously the finer points of different brands like comfortability, stability and affordability, sometimes leading to laudatory. They make numerous pleasing grimaces to the customers which keep on varying, simultaneously accomplishing their task cogently. Also they also tell which sort of shoes are in vogue currently.

Suddenly you see a box falling with a thud from above, precisely in the hands of the boy who is attending you. Again and again the shoes boxes keep on falling from the ceiling central hole. I observed that one of the helpers was putting the shoes boxes on one another, lifting them after making a stack in his hands up to his chin, climbing the staircases laboriously. Again the circle starts of throwing from the ceiling hole on the call of floor boy. I asked them why they didn't arrange the samples in display glass to avoid opening and closing so many boxes and taking them above several times. Then I talked to the frequent climber boy, "You toil more than the other sitting helpers." He told me, "No sir, we work day wise in rotations. but today is my turn." (aaj mein fuss raya hoon).

80. Mischiefs

Childhood's mischiefs are charming to remember, they will make your mood twinkle. It is said that the future of a prankish child is always bright and these devilries are the fundamentals to a growing mind. ln those days I lived in the rear suite of a hired house. A lad, Manjit, from a village who happened to be the nephew of my landlady often made sojourns to this house. The whole house became clamant just after his entry. The vociferous cries of the pinched children, continual falling off things, sudden run of the lads from here and there, were the routine activities. He often started running on boundary walls, hanging from the projections and these things were matters of worry for 'buaji' lest her dear nephew got injured. He climbed to the rooftop, turned off the main valve of the water tank and this made the person sitting on commode screaming for water. Once Manjit turned on the knob of television set until it got free to work and it produced unbearable noise. In a trip he left many things damaged and repairable. Next time I saw him entering from the main gate, he watched the damaged and hanging pedal of the bicycle in the porch of the house. Immediately he yelled, "Listen everybody, I will not be responsible for this already damaged pedal".

He often disturbed the elders taking siesta at noon in the living room by his sudden screams or running between the cots, chasing other children. The upset elders looked at him frowningly, but he ran away when they tried to catch him. At one noon Manjit was agitating an old man who was desiring some nap. Manjit was considering himself as a tractor, making similar sounds, by the actions of his hands he was trying to show as if he was handling a steering wheel and running between the cots without being caught. The old man observed him for some time and waited. Then he saw Manjit was driving himself backwards in a slow pace, in between he was turning his neck to look rear, as the tractors are moved back. In this position when he neared the cot, the old man hooked him by his arm and straightened him substantially.

81. Readymade Garments

His job was seasonal; the sugar mill doesn't run throughout the year. Running period was not also constant; it depended on the availability of sugar cane in the area and also on the sugarcane price policy of the government. In which month the crushing of the sugar cane will start? It was also not fixed. Sometimes it was October or November but sometimes it might be extended up to the month of December and operated till March. Sukhu received the full salary only for the period of three or four months. When the mill ran there were hectic activities, a larger system came into form. His duty was mainly at one of several weighing scales which were installed in rural cane growing areas. Farmers brought loads of sugarcanes in their tractor trolleys or bullock carts which had to be weighed twice, once loaded and again after unloading. There raised a heap of sugarcanes around the place from where it was again loaded in trucks to supply to the sugar mill.

From the supply of raw material, the sugar cane from the farms to the weighing scales, lauding into transport vehicles, unloading at the crushing chain, passing through various equipments and grinders and then producing end products like crystallized sugar, molasses and bagasse all activities were the part of a big operation. Sukhu remained busiest throughout this period due to different duties he performed. When crushing stopped and the mill became inoperative, Sukhu had to seek other occupations. Last time when I met him I asked what he was doing. He told me that during the off season he had tried many assignments like private manual jobs at various establishments. But now he had started his own clothes shop. He also uttered with dampening spirit that he had initiated a clothes shop but it was turning into a readymade garment boutique. I enquired about the reasons. He said, "The fabric I bought came out artificial. Clients buy the cloth, get it stitched, wash, prove it artificial and return; again I had to sell them stitched." I empathized with the predicament of Sukhu.

82. The Property Dealers

The decade of nineties witnesses a spurt in real estate business, a number of people adopted it and there were property dealer offices in every street that resulted in mushrooming numerous new colonies, authorised or unauthorized. Whoever had nourished a desire to settle in a city, that time proved congenial to realize such dreams. An exodus from the villages to the towns took place in large numbers. Several people were indulged in this business like the colonisers, agents, sub agents, professionals, amateurs, investors and middlemen etc. These real estate agents just sold the piece of land on a chart, beautifully designed, showing every amenity like schools, green parks, playgrounds, temples, hospitals, round the clock water and electricity facilities, macadamised roads and sidewalks, but virtually there had been nothing like that except the open farmlands.

These dealers were almost enticers, hoodwinked people by promising profits in a short period or by asserting best locations of the plot. I often observed them doing so. One day the dealer was continually reiterating the client the district secretariat's proximity to the plot which the latter had desired to buy. The client replied that he was not deputy commissioner but a mason. At another occasion the middleman was stressing repeatedly the hospital facility at a short distance, but the client clarified that he was not a cancer patient. People invested in plots and properties by raising loans from the lending institutions, even from the relatives also. In an instance a person asked his relative to support him with a sum of rupees fifty thousands in order that he might buy a plot. The relative inquired him about the total value of the deal. He told his relative that it would be sixty thousands. At this the relative quipped, "Don't be so smart I will buy it for myself."

CHAPTER 17

83. The Tufty Boy

Before leaving to pastures buffaloes stayed for hours at common land which was called 'bakshe'. Where the herders 'pali' used to play games like kabbadi, wrestling and other entertaining antics. Some used to play pranks with each other. The morning time at the common land has always been special. Not only the cattlemen and cowhands but other people also gathered there for amusement. Gags, jests and jokes continued for a long time, till the sun got warmer and the quadruped had to march towards the pastures. In winter season the school started late enough and even the students also entertained themselves with playing activities and often competed with the herders.

One of the herders was 'Dosira' (the double headed) as he was called by this name due to the extra big size of his head. He was not from our village and was staying in some relations. He was specifically brought for the purpose of livestock herding. Dosira never played kabbadi and he was least interested in wrestling but he used to watch others playing. he was also less inclined towards the jesters and mimicking groups, where several people flocked. He himself had developed his own entertaining trick with which he was successful in garnering some amount. He was comparatively a smart fellow.

He used to sustain a 'chotta' the tuft or the maletail. In the morning at the common land he used to challenge other herders that anyone could catch his tuft firmly and he would get it free with a frantic jerk. He played a wager with fifty paise for it. With such pranks he was successful in winning a few rupees daily. One day a sturdy boy accepted the challenge and caught his tuft with extra turns on his fingers. Dosira applied his usual frantic jerk to his head uttering 'le bhi'. What happened, the robust fellow also shouted the same words 'le bhi' at the same time, because the tuft was uprooted and it was in his hand. Thus Dosira lost his chotta (the maletail) and also such earnings for ever.

84. A Departing Girl

Common lands have always been places for numerous activities in a village. In the morning people gathered there with their cattle, before leaving for meadows. They enjoyed their mornings with mutual conversations, gossiping and backbiting. Sometimes they laughed on frivolous issues there, for a long time. Some sorts of sports went on daily that evolved good competitions between teams that were picked on different bases. Generally school going children were on one side and herders were on the other. These teams were also selected on the family and collateral bases. By these challenges tough competitions developed and people got sufficient entertainment dose for the day. At later hours some farmers garnered their grains at the common lands after bringing the crops from the fields. Vagabonds also stayed there in tent covered wagons. Wanderer blacksmiths prepared household things from iron scraps, we watched their women folks billowing the furnaces with curiosity. Their bullock exchange system also added interest.

More interesting things also happened there. The herders witnessed emotionally charged farewells of the married daughters of the village. Such farewells were undertaken with much fanfare. Groups of ladies accompanied the departing girl, who continued to ceremonious sobbing, but the ladies sang special songs at that occasion. Once when such sendoff was taking place, the ladies were marching towards the husband of the departing girl who was waiting near a conveyance with the brothers of the departing girl, a herder who had set his chin on a bamboo stick, was ogling incessantly towards the groomed, preened and well prepared departing girl. The husband of the girl was observing his awkward staring for a long time. At last he went straight to the ogler and asked, “If you are not happy with her going, I should leave her here.” (tu khush nahin to usko yahin chhor jaun).

85. A Pair of Bullocks

A pair of bullocks had been a sign of grandeur for a farmer. I have witnessed a time when people discussed about the bullocks every day, they talked about their races, their alertness, their briskness, even their agility and gait. The status of a farmer was counted on the number of bullock pairs he sustains. Likewise a ploughman always held a higher and respectable rank in society. Tractors and machinery came later, people reared the bullocks in juxtaposition, and they didn’t relinquish their endeared quadruped outrightly. In rice plantation season, in muddling tasks the bullocks were considered more effective, of course it was the most toiling and trading for them also. In evening, milk was served to them as nutrition in order to regain strength, back scratching was also done for relieving pain.

The tractor often became slathered and slippery, causing it to subside and sank in the mud. In the minor tilling also these domesticated animals were more efficacious than dragging the larger machinery. Day to day carrying the green fodder was done with the bullock carts. People lived life with this marvelous animal for a long time. On the festivals these were adorned with beautiful bands, trinkets and bells. Calf races were also organized on carnivals and on off seasons. Brides also used to bring specially prepared coverings called jhool for these bullocks. Whenever someone bought a new bullock, people gathered to see it, gave their comments simultaneously, checked its pace, sometimes its fierceness. There was an adage about bullock buying with additional parameters like, 'Lakha liye lakh ka nilla ek crore, dhola liye bai kae pila diye chhod'. The crux of the matter is bluish bullock valued most in comparison with a bullock of yellowish, whitish and deep brownish complexion.

86. Curious Farewell

Customs of an area has always been peculiar. Generally marriage means to settle down by a bride in bridegroom's house. A few years ago such was the tradition that a girl stayed more at her parents' home more than with the bridegroom. It might have been due to the tradition of child marriage. It took many years for the virtual adjustment of the couple at their own house. After the intervals of four or five months the husband had to proceed to his wife's house to bring her back. The farewell of the girl was also special to be seen. Due to longtime attachment with parents it became very emotional for a girl to leave her ancestral home. All the drama was erected in a girl's farewell with her husband. The girl's brothers accompanied the guest to the bus stop. A group of ladies particularly aunts, sister in laws, young ladies and her intimate friends follow her, singing the farewell songs and the girl continued sobbing and crying due to imminent separation from her parents.

Once a girl was approached to the bus stop with such entourage, at the time of sunset and by all the rituals, so that she may catch the last bus and the whole company returned to their homes after bidding farewell to the departing couple. Unfortunately they missed the bus. The alternate conveyances were not easily available at that time, the transport facilities were also inadequate. She waited for some time at the bus stop, in the hope of availability of alternate vehicle. Seeing no option, the girl with her husband had to return to her house and planned to leave next day. Her mother greeted her again with consolations. But the girl was very upset and she confided to her mother, "Mom, the main difficulty is that tomorrow I have to weep from the beginning." (Kal ne phir shuru se rona padega).

87. Unlocking the Horns

Common land for cattle was the most hectic place on the fringes of a village in the morning. Gradually it was full with the quadruped animals, which were being driven from different cattle sheds. Everyone's buffaloes stayed there before being taken to the meadows. Even a few cattlemen milk their spoilt lactating buffaloes at the congregation. Despite the large number, everybody recognized their livestocks, called them with peculiar names, mostly by their complexions, by their patterns of horns, by lengths of their tails or sometimes by the name of a village from where they were brought. When the herders enjoyed their games without heed the cattle began to move towards the pastures stealthily. The herders had to run to stop the flock intermittently.

The main crisis arose for the herders when the young buffaloes locked horns with each other. When the herders were fully engrossed in their pranks, they began rubbing their heads with each other. While doing this they entangled their horns, they turned berserk and panicky by pushing each other violently. Loss of horn would become imminent. It was not so simple to unlock their horns safely. I have witnessed such scenes several times. There was a robust fellow who had this acume, was called to handle such situations. He immediately tightened his loose clothes and entered the Buffalos' tug of war. By applying ample force and agility he succeeded in disuniting the horns safely. Otherwise numerous young buffalos of "Murra' breed would have become worthless. He came out with a triumphant look in his gleaming eyes. That is why there is an adage, 'Jiske ghar Murra uska bada turra' (rearer of 'Murra' always has a plumy turban).

CHAPTER 18

88. The Sojourns

In nineties I occasionally visited New Delhi for an excursion. My friend Ashish who lived at Janpath often called me and I readily proceeded to Delhi with exuberance. "Let's go to Whimpy" Ashish always uttered these words on my arrival at his home. Whimpy is a posh restaurant in Canaught Palace. I had seen such a restaurant for the first time where you had to serve yourself. The well-dressed staff was there but they were issuing voucher slips and collecting money smilingly, giving due respect to the customers. The charming girls were attending the clients at the service counter just handing over stylishly packed eatables and drinks. You had to pick well covered plastic glasses of water and straws which were placed in a beautiful vertical box. Sausages and jams were already placed on every table. We passed hours on the table of that elite restaurant discussing past heydays and present scenario.

Ashish is a person of conceptual clarity virtually. He has a wholesome answer on any topic. We were sipping our ice-creams on the front table. My eyes were on a guy who was sitting alone on a table. He took out a cigarette consciously from his pocket and hitched it between the lips and then drew a matchbox out from another pocket and lit it. He puffed the cigarette taking his time. Then he stood up to get something to relish from the counter girls wearing shorts and returned to the same table, sipped something with a straw to finish. Again he took out another cigarette and puffed it leisurely. Suddenly a European looking guy emerged from a corner table supporting a bidi, a weedy cigarette, in his tong like fingers and asked for the matchbox to that cigarette puffing person. That fellow was astonished to see a bidi in the hands of a foreigner. He had a beamish look on his face and immediately pulled out a bundle of bidis from his third pocket and flaunted it on the table.

89. A Trip to Narkanda

Narkanda has ever been fancied by me from a long time, mainly on the basis of feedback given by the earlier travelers, and its name is also catchy. But it should be toured in the winter during the snowfall season otherwise it is overall a common place, an apple business centre situated on the Hindustan Tibet highway NH twenty two. On this route we met a young man who was carrying two yaks, which he had fetched them from Tibet. We clicked our photographs for their uniqueness. Transport vehicles make the road congested and somewhere dust hurling. But we were inclined to visit less trampled places, make our way by enquiring the locals and researches. On nine thousand feet height it is a cool place, Apple laden shrubs simply attracted us and we couldn't contain ourselves to take clicks of the apple orchards, reaching between the trees, irrespective of the objections by the orchard owners.

We visited a serene lake surrounded by thick forests, there were hardly any tourist except two young couples.

but the lake was really resplendent. We had to drive forty kilometers to reach river Satluj at a place Luhari on Rampur road. It is a great place where Satluj flows with soothing music between the lush green mountains. On return we detoured Shimla and turned our vehicle on Kufri Chail mountainous road, between the dense forests, large cedar trees touching the sky, the whole route of nearly thirty kilometres is shaded by trees making the trip memorable. Chail is not exception in this respect, a unique place, thickly shadowed by the cedars and pine trees, enough to lower the temperature to chill. Historical palace of Maharajah Patiala is superbly maintained by Himachal Tourism. After the morning stroll in shivering weather of Chail, one of our companions, otherwise nationalistic, talked largely about European lifestyle. Soon we understood the guy wanted to avoid bathing. We got the laughing topic for an hour and he was compelled to have a bath. There are numerous toll barriers on the route. These should be named tatol (search) barriers because they draw substantial amount out of your pocket.

90. A Tour to Nainital

Suffer of nearly 400 km was actually a suffer when we entered Utter Pradesh via Karnal Shamli road. The patch of twenty five km is virtually in dilapidated condition. It was not only full of dust but we experienced jerks and lurches in a great deal. After crossing Bijnor the way is comfortable and soothing. Along the road there are many mango orchards and the whole area is full of lush greenery. There are some lichee orchards along the road when we began driving on the hilly way to Nainital.

The trees are laden fully with lichees. Medium and heavy rain during journey added more beauty. Anyway you have to face some suffering during suffer. The coolness was not so much as we were expecting because the room we hired had ceiling fans that we had to turn on for a comfortable temperature.

As its name signifies, Nainital is a town of numerous lakes, the biggest being the Naini Lake around which the city resides. Overall it is a congested city, the traffic jams are the routine of the day. A walk from 8 pm to 11 pm on mall road which is on the periphery of Naini Lake was really refreshing. A cool breeze coming after touching the gigantic water body was virtually thrilling. It was in stark contrast to the scorching heat of the plains. Among other tourist spots, a cave garden attracted us, a unique structure is carved within a mountain, a number of caves are named as natural habitats for various beasts, and it is adventurous to go through all the caves, where sharp edged stones are protruding at many places. The mountainous road traversed through pine forests to reach at Ranikhet, basically a cantonment town. There is a war memorial, a golf course and also an apple garden but not properly maintained. At that time a cultural festival was being organized and we passed a nice time there. Above all were its soothing atmosphere, lush greenery and zephyrs.

91. Dehradun Escapades

Dehradun and its adjoining areas always attract me. Its semi hilly landscapes, its lush green forests, its heavy rains and of course its fruits especially lichee captivate me. Driving through Kalesar Forest Range is really thrilling. There is never a vehicle in large numbers on this straight and beautiful road, then comes Ponta Sahab a spaciously settled city along Yamuna river bordering Uttrakhand. Just after entering Uttrakhand there starts a picturesque road along a river, then begins a lengthy bridge on Asan Barrage, a water body, all contribute to a memorable journey.

You will traverse many mango orchards along the road, from Ponta Sahab to Dehradun, there are trees which remain covered with beautiful flowers. Dehradun has numerous educational institutes which are of national fame. Its schooling is ever famous globally. Another thing is said about Dehradun is that despite its continual rain it is never effected by floods. There is an adage about Dehradoon, 'heavy raining here, floods far somewhere'. It's also insusceptible to mist, fog and heat waves. We, a group of friends often visit Dehradun and other places on higher altitudes. Dhanaulti is our favourite station for outings.

During such visits an offer came for the purchase of a piece of land from an acquaintance in the vicinity of Land Asia City on the fringes of Dehradun at an attractive price. I saw the location really bewitching, beautifully surrounded by sal forests and that contributed in confirming the deal. After one month my friend Mr. Kalra who applies the principle of 'Money saved Money increased' also showed his inclinations and bought a patch as a tough bargainer. Now we often plan to erect suites as holiday homes on these patches of land at Dehradun if our ships come home.

CHAPTER 19

92. Peals of Laughter

There is a Chinese proverb 'If you don't have a smiling face, don't open a shop'. Yes, smile opens the gates of progress, it makes you acceptable, social, lovable and prolific. Smile and laughter is contagious, spreads from one face to another and there evolve an atmosphere of pleasure and gladness and that pushes away pain and suffering. Performance and productivity is enhanced wherever people adopt such attitude. Physically also your health improves, your more muscles activate, causes beneficial glands secretion. Even memories of laughing are soothing enough. But it should be kept in mind there should be smile, chuckle, chortle, guffaw and hilarity, not in any case derision, brickbat, mockery, scoffing and contempt. It is said that laughter breaks out on the incongruities of life. Man laughs upon himself and when he correlates himself to a funny situation. In the morning, after brisk walking, people sit together, get doses of laughter on trifle matters, and that is the surety of a fine day later. I watch more people assemble there where peals of laughter are erupting and naturally that attracts attention of the morning walkers on the serpentine strip. Seeing them laughing a beamish smile fleets upon their faces also.

But laughter is not sustained by everybody. There are such guys who turn a serious situation into entertaining one with their guts. On the opposite there are such people who carry all the burden of seriousness every time. I noticed a person whom people were trying to avoid in the morning for he drags every issue towards urgency and that tends to grave situations. He might drag you in such discussions in which you are least inclined. He starts from present but speedily marches towards the past and not historical past but mythological past. In a refreshing morning he jumps to the irrelevant matters like mores and manners, customs and costumes of a particular era. Everyone begins to think to leave towards home. One found a remedy to come out of it and created a lighter moment. He said to the serious looking guy, "please lend me your wailing face, I have to attend a mourning ceremony." At this the situation again plunged into hilarity.

93. The Migratory Labourers

At noon all sorts of workers and pedlars assemble at Parallel Poles. They are in a relaxing mood there; even stretch themselves on the horizontally laden electricity poles, exchange views on their mutual callings there, under the shadowy trees. I always enjoy talking with such people. They chuckle and chortle on the employer and other people they deal during the day and also share how much they have earned till that time. They relate amusingly the hardships they face in their professions and also the difficulties they encounter in availing a shelter. Generally these are migratory labourers who lived in huts on the outskirts of the city. A few of them are living in rented rooms of dilapidated conditions where the owner is least interested to provide minimum amenities for these poor people and just visit them to collect the monthly rent.

It is very unfortunate that despite their prolonged stay from home, they are not successful in constructing their own houses. I asked them their names. One was Rinku and the other Mangal as two of them told me. I asked them from where they were and where they lived at that time, how much they had to work and their earnings. Mangal talked more and he said he was from Moradabad near Badaun. Earlier he stayed in a shanty but now he is living in a rented room with other workers. I said, "Mangal, it is a promotion". He smiled grinningly. He told me that he bought and sold trash and was able to make nearly two hundreds daily. He complained about the paucity of entertainment, particularly Bhojpuri films which he used to watch at Panchkula where he worked earlier. There is a theatre in Panchkula where you can see Bhojpuri films throughout the year. I wanted to know some names of Bhojpuri movies he had seen. While proceeding to his pedaling cart he just mentioned one name, 'Pyar karela himmat chahi.' (love is daring). A dashing name!

94. A Group of Retirees

I often sit with a group of retired persons and pass time with them. They relate their experiences of their past services, often swank about the disobedience shown towards their bosses, and simultaneously narrate how he made his subordinates subdued, how they passed time jovially with their colleagues. They discuss about the inaccessible stations and hardships they faced to reach there. Some of them share the merry makings, a tour, travellings, staying at different places, hospitality they received. Again and again they reach their villages and elaborate past games, the famous sportspersons of that era, and their sustained hegemony in a game for a particular period and more of gluttonous habits of some people which are common and boring in this age when people are figure conscious and balanced diet takers. They argue upon politics, often leading to heated exchanges, they talk about the popular leaders of their time comparing them with the incumbents and always judging the older ones better but hardly highlight their particular performances. They repeat such things again and again and all enjoy the same material. Why don't they get bored, I concluded dementia may be the factor. They hardly remember what the topic was yesterday and they continue thrilling on the same topic for several days. It is good for time pass.

There are two or three widowers among them and often debate turns towards them, the company takes it entertaining enough. These widowers share their discomforts, their loneliness without the life partners. The other companions put forward various options and also proposals for remarriage with widows living in similar circumstances, but in a lighter vein. I overheard one of them apprising an eagerly listening widower about the 'Remarriage.com' a website who entertains such curious people.

95. The Milk is Special for You

"This milk is special for you." the milkmen generally say while pouring the milk from a small can. When you turn your back they fill it again from the bigger drum and sell it to the next doorstep by making it special again. They start early, hang heavily made milk drums on either side of the motorbike after filling them with milk from the collection centres. Their bikes are also peculiar, the roaring sound vroom, vroom can be heard from a faraway distance and hardly need horn to blow to call the customer out. They don't have supporting stand and sustains it on the metal barrel dangled on both sides. They buy milk on the basis of fat contents and pay accordingly. But on the delivery no framework is adopted and persistent grumbling may be overheard of the buyers. On the part of the milkman, repetitive assertions of purity comes as rhetorics, like he has brought it directly to you just after milking the buffaloes and nobody supplies it as pure as he does. They often mingled with the housewives and exchange considerate remarks.

In the morning many milkmen halts at Parallel Poles. There they exchange courtesies as well as milk. They take tea and some of them are fond of relishing Balusahi, a sweet like the shape of a hoof of donkey. Today one bargained the half drum of milk with other. But there were no parameters of fat measurement. One of them took a little milk on the palm and tasted it and declared the fat contents 42 and the seller accepted. Thus the deal was done. Other people got entertainment on their patterns and procedures.

96. The Parallel Poles

I like the place Parallel Poles, yes the Parallel Poles, I am giving this name to them, a respectful name, an example of entrepreneurship, an occupation with limited resources.

I am talking of the makeshift tea stalls on the roadside. How they have managed the things? it is simply marvelous, how a line of work may be initiated with a scanty capital? They simply defy the government extensive planning on giving employment, they stand on their own. What we see, the stall, literally, had been a pulling cart previously, its wheels no longer run due to dilapidated rims and flatted tyres, it is covered by the rusted metal sheets. Doors are also hinged, to be latched and locked for security purposes. What's more catching are the parallel poles, a finer sitting arrangement for the customers. I don't think these are purchased from anywhere and might be thrown away electricity poles. They set two half poles horizontally on the stacked bricks in parallel position facing each other and that serves the purpose of chairs and tables.

What they prepare, what they cook, is done in open, in front of you and also on your specifications. They may be seen doing their work with smiles and often humming a song and simultaneously welcoming their clients with warmth. These are not like the so called standard hotels where 'customers are restricted to enter' are tagged on the kitchen door. Their regard to the client is full of warmth. So many people like the workers, the vendors, the pedestrians, the students and many others visit the Parallel Poles to savour the sapidity of tea and other things. By gathering at the Parallel Poles, people have established good mutual rapports and often share their feelings, consult each other on several issues. Affableness in their mutual relations is poignant enough not to be seen elsewhere in the entire business world.

CHAPTER 20

97. A Man of Clout

Sometimes we consider someone a very influential person, a man of clout but generally the actuality is other way round. He may seem in such disposition that others reckon him well connected and powerful enough. He builds such aura around himself by his lofty talks and distinct lifestyle. Gags and brags also play their part in constructing such a prominent personality I am talking of a person whom we called pradhan due to his over involvement in political activities. We often saw him visiting the town and on return narrating the tales of his hospitality at a minister's house. How the minister gave him respect. He often asserted that the mantriji never denied him for anything.

In the rainy season paddy requires abundant of water and regular allotted water hours aren't sufficient for the paddy crop, which is always hungry for irrigation A rain shoot is required from the canal for extra release of water. For this I have to apply in the irrigation department at the district headquarter. But it is not installed without the recommendation of the minister. I approached to the pradhan in order to get favour of the minister. The pradhan agreed to help me in this matter and both planned to visit the minister at his house in the capital city. The next day we embarked on a bus and were successful in getting seat. I bought the tickets for both, of course pradhan also offered to pay for tickets and I noticed he inserted his index finger in his shirt pocket. But I politely refused for it, reason being, he was travelling for my task. We reached at the capital, hired an auto rickshaw up to the minister's residence. The pradhan again inserted his index finger in his shirt pocket, but again I thanked him for the courtesy offer and paid the auto rickshaw fare.

An attendant arranged our meeting with the minister, and we entered the drawing room where he was sitting. The pradhan wished him with folded hands, I followed him in the same gesture. He began forwarding his own requests after apprising him the political situation of the village; he went on urging for his personal things, sidelining mine i. e. the rain shoot issue. At the end of the meeting he just casually talked about my task and the minister also didn't take it in a serious manner. He bid the minister adieu with folded hands; I also followed the exercise in the same way.

It was late enough and we stayed in a lodge. We preferred dinner at a distantly located hotel. We took the meal and again at the payment counter the pradhan repeated the index finger insertion, without actually paying anything. Anyhow I again incurred the expenses. I was not satisfied with the mission completion and the pradhan was reluctant to bear even the partial expenses. On the check out in the morning, he retreated once more and I myself paid the bill of lodging and of having breakfast. I was getting irritated by the way the pradhan was inserting the index finger in his shirt pocket, for everybody knows, bucks can't be extracted by a single finger, but he was habitual to do so. I paid the auto rickshaw charges. We mounted a bus to return home, but just before the leaving, I clambered down, apprehending earlier behaviors of the pradhan, pretexting urgent work and would return the next day. At least he should travel by paying for his own fare.

98. The Scrooge

A miser's hoarding cannot be used in his life time; he doesn't believe in consumerism and not permit anyone to consume his cache. It is not only strenuous but impossible to extract money from a scrooge. No stratagem can transform his thinking pattern. Only greed can hoodwink a miser, so called money multipliers and tricksters often entangle them. They become stickier when a friend or a relative expect an amount for a period, because they don't hope any interest or addition. My friend often talked of his maternal uncle and his wealth. To be more precise the uncle was an interest monger. He lent money in his village on high interest rates. He kept jewelry; livestock etc. as surety, and didn't have much faith on a person's promise.

My friend who was living in a rented house in a town, planned to construct his own house, expecting monetary help from uncle. He accomplished the work of foundation, damp proof course in a short time. Then he approached uncle's village in a buoyant mood, with full expectations of monetary cooperation. The uncle entertained him with courtesy but when he disclosed his intentions about monetary assistance, the old man, a shrewd fellow responded to his demand, "Son, I am ready to perform as a labourer, even for six months, but there is no spare money." (bhanje, tagari chahe chh mahine karwale, pisa ek ni).

99. The Tightwad

If a penny pincher is in your company, he is very much beneficial to you also. He saves not only his money but also of the whole company. He avoids extravagances and continues reminding all of you. A friend of mine is an embodiment of such traits. Generally such demeanor becomes irritating but largely this guy is an amazing fellow. You know a miser is mentioned in many meetings. Without him our outings become boring and draggy, even his doings also develop into interesting discussions. Once we, a group of four friends were visiting Musourie and also Danaulti, a newly developed hill station on higher altitude. We kept a certain amount in a common pool. We halted at a hotel to dine. Three of us moved towards the dining tables, took our seats under the open shed and waited for the serving boy, but my calculative friend proceeded straightway towards the receptionist to enquire about the rate of chapati and asked the peculiar question, 'lalaji, Kitne paise fulka', as was the usage before eighties. We laughed a lot.

Just before Musourie the traffic police stopped us for inspection of the vehicle papers. They found that the emission document of our car was not updated, so the chalan was imminent. My friend tried a settlement with the policeman. By insinuations I said to him, get it done up to 200. He came to us after giving just rupees twenty, we were just flabbergasted on his deal. A few years back we were visiting Golden Temple. One of us who was holding the common amount, bought six hankies for each one from a shop outside the Golden Temple to cover our heads, as is the custom for entering. He got them half the price of general rates. But when the tightwad fellow came to know about this spending, he uttered with a browbeating look, "We would have acquired them free inside the temple, and you just squandered the common pool." (bhiter muft hi na milain thhe, kyun seer ke pisse ka nash thha dhiya).

100. The Tutorials

Tuition has become tutorials, a big profession, business and even companies. No other occupation has flourished like the profession of tuition. Some of such establishments have launched their IPOs and stepped into share market. There was a time when a teacher considered private tuition some sort of degradation and degeneration. Now there are such teachers who feel proud by associating themselves with renowned tutorial groups. Total mechanism of teaching has transformed. The teachers have transfigured themselves into money hunting professionals. Ostensible ultramodern and high tech classrooms overstuffed with students have just turned into money churning centres. Tuitions had been in earlier times also but sparsely. The teachers taught tuition in smaller groups not more than of four or five students on scanty fee. Initially I thought tuition is needed to a weaker student.

When I was studying mathematics at graduation level, I observed some of my classmates visiting a professor's home after the college hours. I enquired more about this type of extra class. They elaborated me all the matter and its advantages and also about the merriment they undertook. I took it interesting enough and joined them. We were a group of five classmates. The professor, a highly learned person taught us in semi arch sitting, We all sat on square stools of wood and the Sir on the diwan, a half bed structure. It was the winter season and the teacher covered himself partially with a quilt. It was also a matter of routine that a cup of tea was also served to the teacher by some family member in the midst of teaching. The professor while grasping the cup, used to ask us for tea for courtesy sake. We politely refused the offer daily. One day we all decided that if Sir offered us today we would not deny but accept the tea. The teaching started, in the same way a cup of tea came, the teacher offered us like earlier times. But today we all collectively said, “we will take, Sir.” The teacher saw us astonishingly and uttered, “stop thinking about tea, just study.” (kya karoge pad lo).

CHAPTER 21

101. Sportsperson

The sportspersons hold a special place in schools. As the toppers are luminaries, likewise players are well known personalities in a school campus. Students emulate them. They are seen enjoying, playing, and getting applause from everybody. The frontrunners outshine themselves and become popular in a short period. One of the reasons is that children show more inclinations towards games than study, they fancy more about playing than reading and choose their heroes from among the leading sportspersons. As I remember studious students, in the same way I recall the notable players from my school.

He was a best attacker in volleyball and best hitters are also best blockers likewise. When he pounced upon a set ball, the players across the net had to flatten themselves to defend the shot. He was popular enough in school and students fancied to play like him. But it is ironical enough the sportspersons are generally lagging in their studies. Yes Dharmi, my school mate is a best illustration of this travesty. He knew the counting in English up to fifteen, so that he might handle game score properly. His prime time passed on playground and his knowhow of mathematics was also far behind.

Our mathematics teacher was illustrating theorems that day and my observation upon theorem is that it is more legal phenomenon than the mathematical. It is not to be solved like other numerical problems but there is always to prove something like in a lawsuit. That day the teacher drew two identical diagrams of two equilateral triangles on the blackboard naming triangle ABC and triangle DEF. His focus was on Dharmi to make him understand. The teacher proceeded forth step to step, equalising angle A and angle D, likewise other angles and sides of both the triangles. In the end the teacher, looking towards Dharmi declared that it is proved now both triangles were completely identical. What Dharmi quipped, "Sir, it was clear from the beginning." (shuru se hi deekh rahi thi). The teacher beat his forehead.

102. An Authoritative Entry

When the government has banned corporal punishment in schools, a teacher has to adopt verbal power and sometimes coercive enough, to pacify the riotous students, otherwise in earlier times when the teacher entered in the class he was generally seen twiddling a cane in his hands and that was sufficient to put in order not only one class but the adjoining classes also. First day entry in any class does matter and that will decide the peace for the year. The first day of eleventh class has always been special, not only for the students but also for the teachers. The students are apprehensive enough to judge the teachers; they observe every minute thing about the tutor, his address, his style and what not. Students are chirpy, perky and coltish that day, they are relieved from the last year's burden. Their mind remained empty for a few months, are meeting the older friends energetically with fervor, some new scholars are also added.

One wants to establish some command and hegemony in the class, seeks such opportunity on the first day. Other wants to highlight himself to leave some initial impression. All things contribute to such developments that the teacher have to prepare himself accordingly to face the challenge competently. Teachers also try to throw good impressions upon the students. Some lectures on maturity and responsibilities and how they have to behave in the coming times. But main motive remains how to maintain discipline in class and there remain conducive atmosphere of teaching and peace for them. Some try to bully the students by making special gestures. I remember a young enthusiast turbaned teacher's first day in class. He started his address screwing the vertical tips of his moustaches, "I don't want any bloodshed in this class." (Dekho mein yahan koi khoon kharaba nahin chahata). What an impression!

103. Efforts by Teachers

The teachers tried hard to teach when there was majority of illiterates. People deprecated going to school and learn. They preferred their children to adopt ancestral professions. The farmers engaged them in cattle herding when they should have gone to school and they happily took the rearing stick. Another thing was that there was a feeling of terror among the children about the teacher's ruler. Corporal punishment was prevalent in those days. It was also one of the reasons for slow growth in literacy rate. Whoever was going to school had a constant dread of teacher's thrashing. School education was also considered unnecessary for a long time because only agriculture generated employment largely. Nonetheless the teachers applied every method to bring the children to school and make them refined citizens. It was very hard to keep the flock together for a teacher in older days, what to talk about teaching.

Truancy prevailed largely, students searched new ways, exculpations to abstain themselves from studying. Assumed illness was general explanation by a student to the teacher to avoid thrashing next day. Some of the truant scholars used to hold onions under armpits and sit under the sun for some time. It was believed that it would increase the body temperature and one would have good excuse for abstaining from school. But I am not sure it worked or not. Our primary teacher, an impressively moustached person was dominant enough. Children remained terrified due to his authoritative demeanor. It was impossible for anybody to remain absent from his class. Nonetheless he was a good planner, beside a teacher. He had divided the class in three categories i. e. cream, horses and donkeys according to the performances of the students. He kept on promoting the students if anyone showed improvement in studies. Besides these groups, there was a sub category of five pandwas among the donkeys and among these five pandwas there was a Marshal a burly boy. This Marshal was very useful for the teacher in beating the students whenever guruji felt tiredness.

104. Ruralites and Urbanites

There is an African adage that a wise person doesn't know everything but a fool knows. There was a time when a lettered person was not taken seriously, particularly in villages and even became the laughing stock among the illiterates. Of course there were probabilities that he had distanced himself from the bucolic atmosphere and with the passing of time he might unlearn the basic and primitive knowhow of a rural life. But on these parameters he should not be judged a non-practical person or simply a blockhead. Whatever he had learned should also be taken into considerations. Time and again I have observed that in a competition between an urbanite and a ruralist, the ruralist always wins. It is also said that the knowledge makes a person reticent but in general such circumstances arise that he adopts an attitude of taciturnity and stoicism. Whatever he had acquired through studies and practicalities ought not be for a propaganda purpose.

The urbanite never tests the knowledge of a rural folk but the bucolic always tries to fathom the intelligence of his urbanite friend. Such foolish questions are thrown to a person who never lived in countryside or had lived in the childhood, like "Do you know what is 'gyaban jhoti ?', 'what is Jhota buggi?' My friend faced such questions once and tried to translate the above terms to the utmost. He said, "I know, one is a pregnant young buffalo and second is a chariot driven by the husband of a buffalo. Yet he was laughed off because he couldn't tell what was 'khola' and 'ghandli' (the rudest buffalo and its ringing bell respectively).

105. Filmy Craze

There was a craze for films at that time, people often talked about films, their stories, characters etc. Theatres also mattered due to their associations to different movies seen in a particular theatre by anybody. People exhibited their inclinations towards heroes and heroines. It is evident from the fact that many have christened their offspring's name after their favorite thespians of that time. Some covered long distances to watch the first show of a movie. There were only three theatres in my town when I was doing my graduation. We tried to do away the work of watching new movies in first three days of their projections. After attending first three periods we marched towards the talkie. Often we tried to make sure our attendance in fourth period in the first few minutes then stepped out stealthily from the back door.

It had been a challenge to see the first show lest someone else elaborate the story of the movie and that might cause diminishing of sensations. The timing of shows remained from 12 am to 12 pm, it might be due to some religious connotations. But the government encouraged watching films because there were concessions in the rates of students' tickets up to forty percent. The licenses to theatres were given in Nehru's reign and Atalji opposed it in a debate in parliament by saying "There should be hospitals first in the country instead of the theatres." But Nehruji replied Atalji politely, "Theatres will be started first and with that earning hospitals will be provided." Anyhow it was travailing enough to get a ticket from the theatre window just like winning a battle. but in my company there were students, proficient enough to extract the film voucher. Some of us even enjoyed a movie repeatedly. That day someone was trying to know the plot of the movie from my friend but the boy quipped, "you just bring ten rupee note I will show you the full movie."

106. Doing a Public Duty

To gain popularity is not so much difficult if you are in the higher echelons of administration, provided you are open ended, receptive and impartial to mingle with people. Even such positions provide you opportunities if you are so disposed. The key post in a district is of a deputy commissioner, he handles not only his own department of revenue but also supervise the spread out administration which works through the subtle ramifications in a specific region. He manages and oversees the activities round the clock. But generally what we see the bureaucrats maintain a detachment and remain disengaged with a common man. Public in general does not know who is at the helm of affairs in a district and largely such officials desire so. And if the public comprehends that the administrator is a benevolent and good hearted person, they throng his office.

I remember such an administrator who was posted in our district. First of all, he was an officer of pleasing personality, a slim and skinny fellow with an impressive voice, his attachment with the commoners was discernible, his office was always full of people with their grievances, and he tried to resolve them satisfactorily. In public or at field duties he was seen with agility, handling public problems heartily. He never displayed himself as a bureaucrat who is indifferent to public causes, but associated and hobnobbed with a layman, people recognized him as person, one of them, among them.

He talked with illiterate farmers and labourers in their dialect, developed cordial relations with communities. Once he launched a drive to uproot the congress grass which was causing harm to health, he participated himself, supervised personality in this exercise. At one place women workers were doing this work, he reached there to enthuse, to persuade them to do speedily. The workers didn't know him. Seeing obliquely one of them uttered, "Are you deployed as deputy commissioner here." (tu ure dc lag rya). The gentleman replied politely, "yes gracious lady, I am a deputy commissioner of this district."

107. The Bragger

We entertain guests but in some sense guests have always been entertainers. Curious things are presented from them to invoke interest in the listeners. A guest is a person with some special privileges, the listeners always have to assent to his claims and stories, be they true or untrue and of course half heartily in the latter instances. Authenticity gathers callousness from the hearers, reason being its repeated nature and commonness. It is said that fiction is always attractive than reality and if a guest is a fabricator, he will certainly hold more attention than a realistic guy. If you are not detecting his lies he will drag you in a utopian state where you will see fancied things that you have cherished earlier. At another instance, if you are fully aware that the gentleman is serving the white lies, you will stealthily smile and even chuckle and chortle. At least there is nothing to lose in both cases.

Once, Uncle Basau had a guest from a considerably distant place. He had reached Basau's abode late in the evening. The stranger made him acquainted indirectly by mentioning some mutually known persons. Anyhow he entertained him fully with all the hospitalities, as are afforded in a village. The guest was a braggart and a line shooter. He continued talking for a long time and uncle Basau kept acquiescing courteously. But his boasts kept no bounds, starting from the larger possessions, the real estate, and the dignified conveyances he stepped towards pivotal political affiliations. He elaborated numerous instances of being entertained by the top political brass of the state.

Uncle Basau felt weary on his gigantic boasts and blusters in a muggy season. He intercepted and told him to leave such impractical things, nothing can be extracted from them. Uncle Basau said that so long as he had concluded that he would demand bus fare in the morning. He added that he supposed he had dined well and should get a good bath to have a sound sleep and indicated towards the water reservoir and a mug placed on its fence. He also said that he would be served with a paranthha, a stuffed loaf besides mango pickles and curd in the morning. It happened what was anticipated. In the morning, after the breakfast the guest asked for a hundred rupee note. The Uncle reminded him about his speculations of the night and said, "I had truly told you, you would demand for a bus fare." (mein kahun thha tu savere kiraya mangega).

About the Author

The author, Shamsher Kendal is a horticulturist by avocation. As a horticulturist sees the growing plants keenly, here he observes people with a peculiar glance and extracts something interesting from everyone and everything. He doesn't consider that only widely known persons are unique and different but a common man, a layman and even a down to earth guy carries things which are so special, there exist numerous people around everyone worth highlighting. In a specific region people quote them, talk about their doings, their habits, their lifestyles and due to such personalities people get sufficient amusement and percepts. The author has taught English literature for twenty years. Besides he has studied law and journalism at Kurukshetra University Kurukshetra Haryana. The author has studied George Orwell extensively and intensively, and is highly impressed by the great writer.